Angel Eyes

Wildcat Wizard Book 4

Get deals and new releases notifications first via the newsletter www.alkline.co.uk

Bloody Noobs

"Damn, my hat," I cursed as I snatched out a hand to catch it whilst sliding on the soaking grass. Okay, I fell on my arse and got my jeans muddy, but it's better if you picture me making a cool move and grabbing my hat before it lands, rather than it falling in a puddle as I flail about like a landed fish.

Which was how I felt.

I retrieved my hat—Grace is her name—from the puddle, tugged her tight onto my head, then clambered to my feet. "Hurry up," I shouted at the massive wolf-cum-housewife-cum-whatever-the-hell that bounded towards me, then I was off, arms pumping furiously, cursing the rain, the mud, the state of my clothes, the economy, the fact chocolate bars were now so small I always had to buy two, that milk didn't come in glass bottles any more, and life itself.

"Don't know why I bother," I muttered through clenched teeth before I spat out a sod of turf and sprinted for all I was worth.

The wolf, which was actually my numpty of a sidekick, Vicky, housewife from hell and annoying mini-mom most of the time, lurched past me, unconcerned by the terrain or the rain, and I swear she smiled a smug smile as I chased her tail. But canines can't smile, although I wouldn't put it past her as she knew it would wind me up.

"You won't be laughing in a minute," I hollered, but the driving wind and rain was pounding us so hard I doubt she heard. She knew though, knew we were almost out of time, which explains the running and why we were so frantic.

Dawn was less than half an hour away, then the full moon would wane, even if the day promised to be dark and dull and as crap as every other day had been for months during this freaky winter. When the night was over, and day became official, Vicky was gonna be in a whole world of trouble. And I'd be right there, lumbered with a noob of a sidekick, a noob of a werewolf, yet an expert pain in my posterior.

Don't get me wrong, I loved Vicky with all my heart, but she was damn annoying and ever since she discovered she could turn once a month if she so wished, she'd gone out of her way to do so. Meaning, every bloody month since summer I had to get her out of one ridiculous scrape or another as she kept fucking up. She'd learned how to remain sane and to think clearly when she changed, but only just, yet lost control, at least briefly, every time she shifted. Let's just say there weren't many bunnies left in the local area and leave it at that.

Tonight wasn't just her fault though, this was one of those times when crap happened the way it often did when a job seemed too easy. Cerberus again, interfering and causing me grief, and I'd had just about enough of them now. Once again, and this time I was serious, Nathan, the posh twat of a face of Cerberus, had to die. I'd kill him. He promised to leave us alone, leave me alone, yet his goons were after us. I was sick of these games.

Yes, in case you haven't noticed, the weather was making me grumpy. Plus, I wanted my breakfast.

Rain turned to a deluge, visibility cut almost to zero, and I was fighting so hard to keep moving as the ground became a shallow river that I forgot I could have kept myself at least mostly dry if I activated the energy stored in my hat. It could expand a simple shield like an invisible umbrella, but at the moment it had defaulted to keeping the top of my head dry and nothing else.

I tucked my chin in and kept going, the rain horizontal now, Vicky's wolf form nothing but a blurry shadow a few paces ahead. Damn, but she was intimidating like that. I risked a glance behind, and smirked as I caught sight of the two surviving goons, the amateur bitches, flailing about in the mud.

"Oomf." I smacked into something wet and went down in a mess of mud. I wiped my eyes only to be confronted with the tiny wet ass of Vicky, my nose almost crammed somewhere it definitely ought not to be—she was married after all—and also, she was Vicky, and I was me. "Ugh, move it, move it," I ordered, voice muffled by wet, wobbly, muddy bum flesh.

Vicky shook her booty and cackled as I shoved at her behind, pushing myself away across the slick ground.

"You picked one hell of a time to shift," I yelled over the rain.

Vicky tried to gain purchase, got nowhere, and fell flat on her stomach again. "Feeling tired," she whined, then rolled over and winked. "Give me a hand?" She lifted a scrawny arm and I sighed.

"You gotta stop doing this," I moaned, hauling her tiny body up.

"You love it," she said, so damn perky and happy I couldn't help but smile even though I was trying to look gruff and angry. Which I guess I did, what with my long brown hair clinging to my face and neck, my sodden leather jacket, my combats that were sticking to my legs, and general permanently grumpy, what people called "lived in" face.

"I love it more when I'm dry, have been paid, and eaten my breakfast," I grunted as I slung her over my shoulder then patted my pocket to make sure I still had my prize. The book was still there, and would be dry, as good wizard thieves always carry ziplock bags, so not everything was going wrong.

"Vicky?"

She snored, the comedown from her transformation having the usual effect, so I moved as fast as I could and plowed on through the rain, hoping the goons wouldn't catch us, knowing they were having an even worse time of it than me.

The quagmire changed to compact gravel as I made it to a path and sped up, legs like lead, back killing even though Vicky weighed less than a bag of groceries, and I got to the car. I opened the back door, threw her in, and annoyingly she didn't wake up to complain, shut the door, got in the driver's side, and sped off.

Before I hit third gear, the rear window exploded with the sound of gunfire, I was sideswiped, and I broke my nose on the steering wheel.

"Fucking rain," I moaned.

Hi, I'm Arthur "The Hat" Salzman. Welcome to my life. Seriously, you're welcome to it. Take it, I'll even pay.

Wakey, Wakey

Vicky screamed from the cramped footwell in the back where she'd rolled off the seat. I groaned and touched my nose, then yelped—I should have learned by now, but every time I broke my nose I had to touch it, and it always hurt. Sighing, I unbuckled, yanked the Velcro free on my custom pocket, and pulled out my wand.

"Stay here. Go back to sleep," I said as I turned and nodded at Vicky.

"Haha, very funny," she said, eyes widening as she realized she was naked, legs sprawled in a most unladylike manner.

I turned front as she scrambled to cover herself with a blanket; served her right for being a bloody lycanthrope. Noob.

I winced as I shoved the door open and something shifted in my ribcage, but it didn't feel broken so I guess that was good news. What wasn't good news was the black SUV that had hit me. Its tires were screeching as it came to a halt after reversing. As rubber burned, it sped toward me.

Gunshots rang out dully through the rain, so I ducked down, cursed life, the universe, and everything, then forced my will down through my aching arm and into the warm wood of my hand-carved wand. Sigils activated, shining bright umber like a beacon of hope when all was darkness, and I smiled, then sneered, as I raised the wand and blasted a tire. It burst in a most impressive way, and metal screeched, sending sparks flying. It was quite pretty.

The driver overcompensated, the amateur, as he began to slide, and veered off to the right, smacking into a lamppost, resulting in the horn blaring, the car buckled, and air bags activated.

Another shot rang out, trashing the door panel, and I crouched lower then ran around to the passenger side as footsteps splashed across soaked asphalt. Pissed off, and knowing I couldn't get any wetter, I dropped flat and, as the muddy black shoes of a Cerberus goon, what they liked to call Hounds, stopped where I'd been a moment earlier, I let rip with the trusty wand. Power like sick lightning erupted from the tip and disintegrated the guy's foot.

He slumped to the ground and we locked eyes for a moment. "Bad day to screw with me," I growled, readying to explode his head. His eyes widened with fear and pain, and then I let rip.

I looked away as the energy surged and spat from my wand, I'm squeamish like that. Rolling back, I clambered to my feet, stormed over to the SUV, and as two guys half fell from the vehicle, slipping as they tried to run, I shouldered one in the back so he smacked his head on the door and went down. Whirling, I blasted the other one through the open door, but he was fast and I only got a glancing blow to his shoulder.

He turned and fired, but I was already on top of the guy I'd downed, so I used the wand to pierce his brain through an ear. There's no point wasting magic when you don't have to. Then I grabbed his gun, fired a few rounds, hightailed it to the rear of the car, and as the last Hound crouched behind the driver's door I shot out the glass then took careful aim and fired again. Half his face blew off, landing in the dirt on a nondescript road.

Thoroughly depressed, I threw away the gun, hunched my shoulders, and ambled back to my car. The engine was still running, so I turned up the heater, pulled out my phone, made a call to the Cleaner, and put my seatbelt back on.

"Arthur, you could have just driven off," chastised Vicky as she tugged a tiny red sweater over a ponytail pulled tighter than my nerves.

"And you could have shifted a few minutes later and this wouldn't have happened."

"It's not my fault," she moaned, poking out her tongue.

"Whatever. Put some jeans on," I ordered as I glanced in the rearview mirror.

"I'm trying, but I think I've put on weight." Vicky wriggled about as she slid her jeans up, and I sighed.

"Don't start. If you get any more skinny you'll have to buy kids' clothes. Oh, wait, you already do."

"Just shoes," Vicky shouted. Why, I have no idea, but she was like that. "Um, and socks. And sometimes jumpers if they're in the sale."

"Put your seatbelt on," I said, forcing myself to remain calm. We drove off back to the city she called home and where most of my business was centered.

"Do you still have it?" Vicky asked once she was buckled up.

I opened the hidden zipper of my jacket—yes, I like a lot of pockets—pulled out the sealed book no larger than my hand, with a black cover and black pages, seemingly devoid of words but screaming DANGER as it oozed weird magic, and said, "Sure do."

She smiled, I smiled; another job well done.

Deal

"I can do it on my own. I managed fine before you. I'm the bloody professional here," I lectured, more exasperated by the second.

"That's debatable," Vicky muttered from the back seat.

"You want to be put over my knee and spanked?" I asked, glaring at her in the rearview.

"You wish. Let's just get this done. But don't keep me out of the action, Arthur. We're a team."

"Fine, just try to behave, will you?"

"I always do."

I got out of the car, saying nothing more as we'd had this conversation too many times already. Then I had a thought and put a hand out to Vicky as she began to follow. "Hey, what about the kids?" I asked brightly. "Don't you have to get them off to school?" Haha, I had her now.

"It's Sunday, they won't be up for hours. Neither will Harry."

"Harry? You got a new dog?"

Vicky stood on tip-toe and peered into my eyes, or tried to, she still only came up to my chin. "Are you trying to be funny?"

"What? No, if I was, you'd be laughing."

"My husband. Will you please try to remember his name?"

"Sorry, it's just I've called him the Slug for so long."

"Yeah, well, I'm not doing that any more. We're getting on really well and he's even taken up running."

"Ugh. Whatever." We crossed the street, parking not a problem this early in the morning. I shuddered as an image of "Harry" covered head-to-toe in Lycra, sweating and puffing, flesh wobbling as he ran, crowded out all other thoughts.

I was half asleep as it had been a long night, and Vicky was just as zombified since she was always utterly drained after her monthly shift. But Vicky was Vicky, and she'd rather die than skip any action. She was, without doubt, the most intense person I knew. She hated missing out on anything to do with this magic-infested gangster life she had been embroiled in ever since I let her become my new sidekick, something I regretted every day. But she somehow managed to help, even when I thought she couldn't, and her computer skills were second to none, the reason I had got to know her so well in the first place.

She was finally learning the ropes, though. She'd always acted the part, but now she was getting good at this game and it worried me. She'd get herself killed one of these days, and chances were, I'd be dead right alongside her.

I rapped on the door to the tiny cafe run by Candy, owner and super-hot shifter, full of secret desire for yours truly. I wished. Images of the Slug were replaced with images of bouncing boobs and naked bottoms, in no way lessened when Candy scowled at us as she unlocked the door and I caught sight of her plain black work trousers and white shirt with two whole buttons undone.

"What are you smiling at?" she asked as she brushed slightly disheveled curly blond locks from her lovely face. She'd taken a while to warm to me, but I'd won her over in the end.

"Just pleased to see your beautiful face on this otherwise depressing day," I said as I entered.

"What about my face?" asked Vicky before the women hugged and I frowned. I never got hugs, not even a peck on the cheek.

"Exactly." I mumbled.

Candy closed the door, leaving it unlocked, then went behind the counter. The whole cafe was narrower than my hallway, the counter taking up half the space along the right-hand wall, chairs and tables crammed in. But it was comfortable, warm, smelled of coffee, and had become the default meeting place to exchange items for payment with the vampires. Brains, a.k.a. Ivan now usually coming in person for the deal.

"They here yet?" I asked, doing this really annoying thing I kept doing in Candy's company and saying utterly stupid shit.

Candy looked around the cafe and said, "Oh, yes, they're hiding under the table over by the window."

"Just asking. Any coffee?" Ugh, what was wrong with me? Both women stared at me and I scratched under my hat. "It's been a long night, I'm running on empty," I said by way of explanation.

"I'll get the coffee," said Candy, giving me another curious glance like I had several marbles missing.

"Thanks for opening up for us," said Vicky as she leaned on the counter and watched Candy.

"Why so early?" she asked, taking the envelope I slid across the counter and pocketing it. Payment for services rendered, the usual rate.

"Guess Ivan needs his beauty sleep during the day now," I said.

"He's finding it tough to stay awake during the daytime, but can cope with the morning and evening," said Vicky, more in the know because they had spent a lot of time together since discovering they were brother and sister. Long story, read the book.

"Guess that's to be expected." Candy served three coffees and we drank in silence, enjoying the caffeine boost.

The bell rang over the door several minutes later and Ivan entered. Two very large, very goony looking goons poked their heads in and gave me the gangster stare, so I smiled at them. I got the usual blank looks in return then they closed the door and stood out front looking suitably menacing.

"Morning, Ivan," I said cheerily, saluting with my mug.

"Morning, brother," said Vicky, all smiles, still acting insanely excited to have a vampire, werewolf, gangster as a brother. It was like all her Christmases come at once.

"Morning, sister. Arthur. Candy. Can I have an Americano please?"

"Sure," said Candy, and while she made it we took a table.

The usual digital stuff was brought out, Vicky and Ivan confirming the transactions to my account, and hers, had been completed, then I slid the book across the table. Ivan pocketed it without a second glance.

"Thank you. The First will be most pleased. He's happy with the arrangement, Arthur, if you are?"

"I guess. Why'd you get rid of Steve though? Thought he was supposed to give me the details, manage the deal?"

"We no longer felt it necessary. You proved your worth, your trust, no need to complicate things."

"You mean you wanted to save money?"

"Correct. You don't run a successful business by spending when you don't need to."

Ivan was a practical man, was smart, and had done a damn good job of improving the vampires' position since he gained control of the underworld in the city, his influence spreading. He now ran, either directly or indirectly, most criminal activity in the country. He was fair, but he was no fool, and he was ruthless when he had to be. I liked him. He saved my daughter; I could never repay that kind of debt.

"Poor Steve," said Vicky.

Candy placed Ivan's coffee down and said, "Yeah, he's been a nightmare since you gave him the elbow. Moping about the place."

"Business," said Ivan. "Thanks for the coffee."

Candy got the message and retreated. This wasn't for her ears.

"So, I have another job for you."

"What, now?"

"Cool," said Vicky, eyes sparkling.

"Yes, now. Today. It must be today."

"Man, I need to sleep. I'm dead on my feet. You too, Vicky."

"You can rest all day. This is best done tonight. Double the usual rate."

"Fine," I said, not really keen but also unable to turn down a job with such a great payout.

"I get double too," said Vicky, glaring at me, daring me to try to haggle. I'd learned my lesson about that, didn't have the energy.

"Sure, you get double too."

"Yes!" Vicky punched the air. She was such a noob.

"I want you to get—"

The bell rang above the door, and we turned.

A goon fell in with a loud crunch as his face hit the tiles, then the other one crashed in on top of him.

Both dead.

I hate the mornings.

No Deal

"You expecting company?" I asked, eyeing the dead dudes wearily. I heaved myself out of my chair, but I was in no mood for this crap, just wanted a lie down.

"It's becoming an annoying habit," said Ivan. He frowned as his slender, tall frame shuddered almost imperceptibly, but he didn't get up.

I sidestepped the goons and peeked cautiously around the doorway but there was no one there, no sign of the assailant. Ivan was already on the phone calling for a clean-up crew, voice calm and unflappable.

Candy rushed over and glared at Ivan, but she said nothing. When he hung up he fished in his inside jacket pocket, pulled out an envelope, and handed it to her. "I came prepared. This is for your trouble." Candy snatched it, grumbled, then went back to pretending not to listen in.

"You don't seem very surprised," I said, taking my seat.

"Are you in danger?" asked Vicky, all concern.

"It's a minor annoyance, nothing to worry about. Now, about this job."

"Deal's off. You're up to something, I don't want to get involved."

"Not even for double money?"

"No." Like I needed the money. Sure, it was always good to make hay while the sun shone, but I wasn't starving or anything.

"Okay, triple. Final offer. Ask no questions, just do the job. And tonight."

Vicky turned to me hopefully, and said, "I want to build an extension. Please, Arthur."

"Buster's hat! The money you've had from me, you could buy a new house for cash."

"I like it where I am, thank you very much."

I sighed. "Fine, what's the job?"

"Another book. Should be easy."

And it was.

What came after, that's a whole other story.

Home at Last

I dropped Vicky off then took the trashed car to a guy I knew and swapped it out for some bland piece of crap. Feeling the paranoia kick in, I drove around the city for half an hour then parked up outside the new place I'd bought specifically so nobody would know where I housed the Gates of Bakaudif, or one of them at least.

With a final paranoid check, as the bastards really were out to get me, I pulled my hat low, grabbed my gear from the car, put the nonsense of the night behind me, and walked to the front door. Wards were still in place, nothing felt fishy. I got no tickle at the back of my neck, so did the necessaries and entered.

Dead on my feet, I walked straight to where the gate was hidden behind the plasterboard, felt the familiar tingle, and stepped through into my barn. I hauled open the huge doors, the smell of hay and fresh country air beautiful after the stench of the city, drove out in the battered Jeep I'd grown attached to, then closed the doors and headed home feeling the years drop away like dandruff.

Driving through lanes, past herds of cattle and grazing sheep like clouds on grass, and seeing the Cornish countryside in general lifted my spirits, told me everything wasn't so bad and that life was good. The closer I got to home, the happier I became.

By the time I'd parked and crossed the cobbled courtyard as chickens pecked at my feet, I had a genuine smile on my face.

I'd made it home in time for breakfast, something I'd always tried to do, although dinner was the one meal me and my daughter, George, never missed having together if we could possibly help it.

Inside the house, I frowned at the dark and silence, walked through the hallway crammed with books and general tat, and into the open, immaculate, beautiful, clean, and light kitchen.

Sighing, I took off my hat and jacket, put my wand on the counter, then breathed, relaxed for the first time since I'd left the night before to go do this job. Now I had another one, but I decided not to think about it. Time for that later. First, coffee, then breakfast. But where was George? She was usually up by now.

Ah, Sunday, the day of rest. She'd be deep under the covers, catching up on sleep. My head nodded forward and I got a sharp pain in my neck. I'd fallen asleep just thinking of bed.

I shook my arms and legs, jumped up and down a few times and made funny noises to jolt life into my old bones, then set about preparing a feast. After coffee, of course.

Forty minutes later the table was laden. I heard the stairs creak, and the most perfect, wonderful person in the world shuffled into the kitchen looking like she'd had a fight with a tiger and lost.

My daughter. The one ray of light in an otherwise dark, unforgiving world.

"Morning," I said brightly, angling my head to indicate the feast on the table.

"Garumpff," she responded, or something suitably teenage and non-verbal.

"I made breakfast," I said, beaming.

"Urgle," she replied before slumping into the chair, her wavy auburn hair spilling forward, tips soaking up coffee and baked bean juice.

"Tuck in, I made loads." I brought the toast over and sat, inordinately pleased to feel normal.

"What are you grinning at? You look weird," accused George, staring at me suspiciously.

"Nothing. Just nice to see you. Did you have a good Saturday night? Go anywhere cool? Any boys there?" I asked casually, not really interested at all.

"Ooh, subtle. I told you, there's no boys at the moment. I'm too busy."

"Hmm."

"Don't start!"

I held my hands up in protest. "Didn't say a word."

"Good. And yes, I was with Sasha, but I didn't stay long in Faery."

George had taken to calling the land of the fae, Faery, as no human is allowed to know the real name, or utter it. But George, who was, to all our surprise, half fae, had been spending a lot of time there with my faery godmother, and I did not like it one bit. In fact, I hated it. It was dangerous. Fae were sneaky, could be cruel, and played games no human could hope to understand, let alone win. George was my daughter and I worried.

I was worried when she turned up on my doorstep the night her mother died, and I'd worried ever since. I had the gray hairs to prove it. And I loved her with all my heart, and she loved me, and I wasn't used to being loved, even after her living with me for several years.

We fought to begin with. She was sullen and remote, only came as she had nowhere else to go, but I welcomed her, told her what was mine was hers. She never once, ever, took advantage of that beyond what any regular kid would do, let alone one who was training to be a witch then found out she was fae and began to grow in magical ability faster than I'd have liked. Meaning, at all.

"Hello? Earth to Dad." George waved her arms about in front of me, smiling.

"Sorry, need to sleep."

"How was it? Did you get the book?"

"Yep, no problem. Got another job tonight though. But not until after dinner."

"Oh, okay. But by no problem do you mean loads of bad guys, lots of running, lots of nonsense, and Vicky being, er, Vicky?"

"Haha, that's exactly what I mean."

George knew what I did, I never lied to her, often told her all the gruesome details, and she didn't judge, didn't accuse, call me a bad man. Our world was not the ordinary world and we were not, for our sins, ordinary people.

I studied her while she ate, and damn but she was beautiful. Large green eyes, pointed chin, sharp cheekbones, that amazing hair, and a body I never looked at as that would be weird. She wasn't your typical young woman, even apart from the magic. She didn't dress down or follow fashion, often wore pencil skirts with vintage blouses and heels, always classy.

But her mother had been fae, not that we'd known until Sasha told us, so that explained her beauty. She certainly didn't get it from me. But she was still young, impressionable, and prone to being moody now and then, which she probably did get from me. Insomnia will do that to a guy, not that she had trouble sleeping.

"You're weird sometimes," she said with a mouthful of fried egg.

"Am not, you are. I was just looking at you. You're such a good girl."

George's neck flushed but she smiled. "Idiot."

We continued breakfast, just the two of us, and it was perfect in every way. Even when I fell asleep and scalded my nose on a sausage.

Curse My Brain

Beat, I hauled my weary ass up the stairs, did that stupid thing where you hop about trying to get your trousers off, rather than just sitting on the bed to do it, finally got naked, shuffled into the shower, cleaned my scrawny, hard body until it shone pink, then collapsed on the sheets, shivering.

I pulled the duvet up to my chin, shifted about until I had a nice dent in my pillow, got all warm and toasty, and closed my eyes with a sigh, mind empty.

Sleep, the mini-death I longed for every night. So elusive was this glimpse of the final frontier that I often wondered if people were lying when they said they slept all through the night, every night.

Why couldn't I do that? Why couldn't I even get a few hours of peace?

I remained motionless, and each time a thought or worry came to me I pushed it away, forcing my mind to empty and to still. But sleep eluded me. I was exhausted, had been working all night, chased by bad guys, killed quite a few, completed the job and got paid, and yet still my body refused to succumb to what it needed most.

Shouldn't have had the coffee, not that it ever made any difference.

I glanced at the clock only to find I'd been lying there for an hour. This was ridiculous, and damn frustrating. I began to think about Vicky and her newfound gift, or maybe curse. Ever since she'd discovered her link to Ivan, and their shared ability to shift around the time of a full moon, she'd been like a thing possessed. Ivan taught her the rudimentary rules of her lycanthropic metamorphosis, how to maintain that inner sense of self rather than become the animal like most regular shifters did, and he'd helped her deal with it. But she was new to it, had only had a few changes, and didn't seem to be taking it seriously as far as I could tell.

She was setting herself up for a serious fall if she didn't watch it. I'd warned her repeatedly but she dismissed me as being a nag. Me, a nag! That was rich coming from the woman who couldn't say five words to her kids or husband without three being an order.

Thoughts switched to George, and boy was there plenty to worry about there. Concerns about her new life as part of the faery world crowded in, but I caught myself and stopped the thoughts dead. I'd never get to sleep at this rate; this was the last thing I should be doing.

So I repeated the usual routine, stilled my mind, pushed thoughts away, and just lay there, trying not to get worked up about my lack of rest.

Hours later I must have finally dozed off, as when I woke I was starving hungry, the day was dull, dusk mere minutes away, and the house was quiet. Exhausted, I nonetheless got out of bed and dressed in clean clothes. I went downstairs and put some coffee on then found the note from George. She'd gone to visit a friend in Mousehole, a small fishing village that was overrun with tourists every summer and quiet as the grave during the off-season. Just the fishermen in the harbor, and the locals. Nice and quiet how I liked it.

She'd be back for dinner, she promised, about seven, so that gave me a few hours to do whatever I wanted, then I'd start cooking. I decided to make a full roast, it was Sunday after all, and it was traditional. But first, I had some planning to do. Or, I guess, Vicky and I did.

I checked my email and found that Vicky had done as promised and had been hard at work, even though it was a family day for her. She was a whiz with all things dodgy on the internet, the result of years being unable to sleep, just like me, although for different reasons, and was one of the best hackers in the country, although you'd never believe it to look at her with her tight ponytail, her mom sweaters, and her permanent smile and obsession with her two girls. But she'd always had a dark side, craved excitement, and until she'd hooked up with me the way she found that release was by doing dodgy stuff online.

Which was exactly what she'd done for me. For us, I guess. She was getting paid too.

I opened the attachments she'd sent, studied the layouts, the alarm system, the grounds, all the usual stuff, and couldn't see much of a problem. Vicky had already set up a blackout of the alarms, they'd go off when we needed them to, so we wouldn't be caught on camera or trip anything. This joker of a collector, and you'd assume they'd have learned by now, didn't even keep his books in a strong room, but had them in his actual library, on display in ordinary glass cabinets.

Easy peasy.

After that I set about making dinner, tried to get the small TV to play a Buster Keaton short, but, as usual, couldn't get the damn thing to work, so had to wait until George came home. She sighed and smiled when she arrived, but let me chortle away to his antics, rolling her eyes as usual, and then we ate roast chicken, onion gravy, potatoes, veg, and even had Yorkshire puddings too. A perfect evening with my daughter.

Once finished, and the kitchen cleaned until it sparkled, George whipped out a fat hand-rolled cigarette, the only one I was allowed each day, our deal as she hated smoking but I loved it. I pulled aside the full height glass doors at the far end of the kitchen, breached the cold, and stood in the rain, smoking, enjoying every puff.

Then it was time for action.

Gear grabbed, I kissed my daughter, put my boots on at the front door, and stepped out into the courtyard.

My senses were immediately on high alert. I bristled, and if I'd had hackles they would have been raised, but the security lights weren't on, the wards were all in place, and whatever had been here was gone. But something had been here, and the number of people who knew where I lived was very limited, although not as limited as I'd have liked.

I looked up into the dark night as something drifted down. I put out my hand and a single, fluffy black feather came to rest in my palm. Birds? Weird.

Body buzzing with anticipation, I headed back into the urban jungle and the madness it contained. A madness I thrived on, needed, craved more than nicotine.

A Bad Feeling

"That was way too easy," I said, pulling the prize out of a leather satchel to look at it again.

"What do you mean, easy?" Vicky scowled as she wiped at her face, then shook her fingers to get the worst of the mud off.

"I mean, I've got a bad feeling about this."

"You always have a bad feeling." Vicky dropped the bags onto the straw in the barn and pulled out wet wipes and a change of clothes. "If you don't mind?"

"Oh, beg pardon." I turned away while she cleaned herself up a little, used to her ways now. One minute she couldn't care less if I saw her naked, the next she was all coy. I think it was the shifter thing. The closer to a change she was, the less concerned she became with decorum.

Jobs were never like this, something stupid always went wrong since Vicky had started tagging along. Um, actually, all my previous partners had a similar affect, or maybe it was just me. We'd had no issue with the security, I took the silver box without incident, no deadly gasses or poisoned darts, Vicky hadn't screwed up while I was inside the house, and we'd made a mostly clean getaway.

Sure, there was the dog, and the running, and the loss of Vicky's jumper to said dog, and her falling flat on her face in a repeat of the day before, but I'd told her to wear boots rather than plimsolls. But would she listen? No.

Apart from that, we'd got away clean. We'd hightailed it to the portal, come right through and emerged in the barn, and the whole thing had taken two hours start to finish. Weird. Unsettling. Easy.

Bad.

"So, what's next?" asked Vicky, tugging at my sleeve.

"You wanna do something?"

"Sure, it's the middle of the night, no way can I go home and sleep. I'm too hyped."

"Yeah, me too. Let me stash this, then we'll head back, kill a few hours." I stowed the simple silver box, decoration minimal, seventeenth century and worth a small fortune in its own right, after taking another peek inside. The book it contained was so worn the binding was as thin as the paper it held, the leather soft yet cold. It felt almost fluffy, like eiderdown, and the magic screaming at me from within made me certain that keeping the book closed was the smart thing to do. And, for once, I did the smart thing.

It wasn't just magic inside, it was something else. Something beyond my knowledge, almost spiritual, hinting at things mortal man ought not to know.

Whispering of the secrets of existence itself, of devils and demons and angels and gods and I wanted no part in that. I just wanted to be paid by Ivan and have done with it. Whatever Mikalus, vampire First, founder and resurrected leader of the undead, wanted with it was his business. Maybe it had been part of his collection long ago, the collection I seemed to be gradually restoring for him. Maybe not. I didn't know, or care.

I closed the lid to the box, locked it securely in one of the ward-protected hidey holes dotted about the barn, and turned.

"You can stop pretending you aren't looking now," I said to Vicky as she suddenly found her fingers of utmost interest.

"Wasn't," she said, cheeky smile giving the game away.

"Come on, we deserve a treat. Big payday in the morning, then maybe have some time off?"

"Sounds good to me," she said as she skipped after me and we stepped through the portal back to the city.

Just before I went through, I swear I saw something fall through the air, almost like a feather, but I dismissed it. Just a flash of light from the portal playing tricks on me.

Wombling Free

"You need anything?" I shouted into the phone.

"I'm good," came the grunt of a reply. Metal clanged in the background. I could almost taste the sweat.

"Okay if I bring a friend?"

"Ugh," came the reply.

I hung up.

"We're all set," I told Vicky.

"For what? Is it a party? I haven't been to a party in... Gosh, years."

"Yes, it's a party."

"Cool." Vicky did her mom-jig, I checked nobody was watching, but then she stopped and turned back to me. "It isn't, is it?"

"No."

"Why'd you say it was?"

"Because my sole goal in life is to make you happy."

"No need to be sarcastic, Arthur, that's just mean."

"You wanna come or not? You could always go home," I said hopefully.

"No, I want to come. Um, where is it we're going again?"

"You'll just have to wait and see. Think of it as a surprise."

I'd parked up in a quiet part of the city, where warehouses gave way to not much of anything. The dying edges of a slowly crumbling city in an eroding country in a decaying world. It didn't matter how many new buildings went up, how much steel and shine there was at the heart of the metropolis, this city was the same as all others. A massive gap between rich and poor, the most needy parts neglected, the old houses, warehouses, and factories left to disintegrate by owners and landlords who'd given up and moved somewhere warmer and cheaper, meaning anywhere apart from here.

The outskirts were a warren of concrete-lined canals giving way to marshland where the runoff from the main river was diverted. Where once it supplied the factories, now it was stagnant, fetid, everything blocked up and fouling the air. Nobody came here apart from teenagers to drink somewhere quiet, graffiti artists to practice their craft, the junkies, the homeless, or the merely desperate not long for this world. Even a few prostitutes that had sunk low and succumbed to the darker side of man's perversions.

Ivan had cleaned up most of that though, had looked after the women, tried to control the addicts but maintained a firm grip on the heroin trade, eliminating the scammers and the competition, promising to improve things, but saying in no uncertain terms that there would always be drugs and always be addicts. He was, after all, a gangster. The uber-gangster, as far as I could tell. At least in his version of that world.

I had my own version, and liked to think I was pretty high up in it. Certainly I was one of the best wizards in the country, undoubtedly the best thief of magical artifacts, and adept at plenty of other, less than wholesome interests.

We walked under vast bridges, the motorways elevated over the swamps and canals, past shanty towns of homeless, kept a discreet distance from abandoned warehouses where the moans of the addicts and the screams of the mad rang out loud. Vicky clung to me as reality got darker and juicier, but I liked these places, felt at home because this was real, this was honest. This was life. It made me appreciate what I had, what I'd once been, and the life I'd made for myself. I hadn't done half bad, had I? Even before George there had been a turning point and I'd pulled myself up from the gutter, got my act together, and made a comfortable, if interesting, life for myself.

"Arthur, where are we going?" Vicky whispered as we passed a group of feral looking kids spraying tags on a stanchion whilst passing around a fat joint that sweetened the rancid air.

"Not far now, the door is around here somewhere." I tried to get my bearings but it all looked the same. I kept an eye out and soon found a bright piece of art with a familiar sigil in sunshine orange and knew I'd found what I was looking for.

"Is that a dog?" Vicky gasped, grabbing for my jacket as something mangy and huge loped off into the shadows.

"No, so stay close." She did.

"Sometimes I think you're from another planet. Who would come here to unwind?"

"Here we are," I said, smiling.

Vicky looked around, confused. "You said there was a door. I don't see one. Ooh, ooh, is it a magic door."

"Nope," I said, my grin getting wider, and it may have even been a slightly mischievous one. "We're standing on it."

We both looked down, me with anticipation, Vicky with a frown.

I bent, muttered several words, and light shone around the rim of the manhole cover. I hauled it off, and said, "After you."

Vicky punched me hard on the nose, making my eyes water. Charming.

Grungy

All cities have sewer systems. Some are vast, some are ancient, most are kinda fun. I'm not talking about the image you have in mind of low tunnels with liquid shit slowly passing by as you hold your nose and search for the nearest ladder to climb back to the street, I'm talking about the real magical world beneath old cities.

The original sewer systems were things of beauty, built centuries ago in many cases, improved upon by the Victorians, and then mangled by modern city planning departments, much of the old stuff left abandoned or bricked up in the name of progress.

This was where we were going. To the maze of centuries-old tunnels and cavernous rooms designed to take away the waste of the masses back when everyone had an outside toilet, and running water and drainage were still fairly new to most folks.

At the base of the ladder, I grabbed a heavy duty rechargeable light from a deep recess in the wall, left for guests if they knew where to look. Once we'd navigated the modern sections, thankfully tunnels that dealt with water runoff so the city didn't flood rather than anything too stinky, we passed through a series of impressive, and dry, brick built tunnels easily thirty feet high. At junctions there were ornate arches and detailed brickwork that was awe-inspiring, the craftsmanship outstanding and shocking—you just didn't get such considerations for utilitarian construction in the "modern" world.

As I shone the torch at one particularly impressive arch with staggered brickwork and even worn faces carved directly into the brick in bas-relief, Vicky whistled.

"See, told you it was beautiful."

"But it's the sewers. I thought we were going to do something cool."

"We are. I hope you had your energy drink."

"Huh?" Vicky teetered forward on tiptoes and squinted up at me in that way she thought intimidating but always made me think she'd topple over and I'd have to move and let her fall on her face. "What are you up to, Arthur Salzman?"

"Something to burn off the high. Something so we can sleep. Plus, I haven't seen my buddy for a few weeks so want to say hi."

"Ooh, so mysterious." Vicky planted herself back down, but I knew she was dying to find out what this was all about. She loved mysteries, part of the reason why she had always been so keen to hook up with me.

"Come on, it's not far now."

I led the way, shining my own torch with one hand, holding the powerful industrial light with the other, and we entered a large square space, its true height lost to darkness. This was an old cistern, now bone dry, with a series of rooms off it with large steel doors controlled by a series of weights and pulleys that had been modified by the current occupant.

They were all closed, but a sliver of light spilled from underneath a few of the steel slabs, and you could certainly hear the grunts.

Vicky took a step toward the source of light and noise, turned and looked at me, then rushed back. "Is someone keeping animals down here? What for?"

"Haha, no, nothing like that. You'll see." With a smile, I approached the barrier, grabbed a pipe leaning against the wall next to it, rapped loudly on the door in a specific sequence, and stepped back, dragging Vicky with me.

Chains rattled like the anchor of a vast ship being hauled up, metal ground against runners, and the door began to rise.

Hot air rushed out to greet us, and then the stench hit. It pushed us back like a physical force, and Vicky gagged. I took it in, let it become part of me, as there was no fighting it and no escaping it if you wanted to enter this domain.

"Just go with it, and don't pull faces. He doesn't like that."

"Who? Who doesn't?" Vicky peered through the now raised doorway, squinting against the light shining out, a secondary precaution so my friend could check who'd come calling whilst blinding you.

The light was adjusted, revealing a monstrous silhouette, and then I was grabbed in arms any gorilla would be jealous of and a gentle voice said, "Arthur, so good to see you." Alfonse released me so I risked a breath, pleased to discover no ribs were broken, although my ribcage hurt like hell, probably from the action the previous night, and then Beast turned to Vicky.

Fair play, she held her ground, then my buddy said, "Ah, I see you brought me my supper. It'll do for a snack, I suppose."

Vicky ran, but I grabbed her sweater and she bounced back into my arms. She squeaked.

"Thought some fresh blood was just what the doctor ordered," I said, glaring at Vicky.

Alfonse, known as Beast to friends and enemies alike, lumbered back into his cave, and I carried a protesting Vicky in under my arm while she squealed, and kicked her legs.

Fun times.

Muscle Time

"Put me down, put me down," Vicky screamed as she struggled like a bagful of sentient potatoes.

"Where d'you want her, Beast, straight in the pot?" I caught Vicky's gaze and winked at her then placed her on her feet.

Alfonse laughed then said, "Stop winding her up, Arthur, she looks dangerous."

Vicky squared her shoulders and stepped away from us, her features contorting as she went from fear to anger to defiance and then, as usual, curiosity. "You, um, you aren't going to eat me?"

"Haha, of course not, little lady. Arthur was just pulling your leg."

"Yeah, Beast only eats animals with some real meat on them. Vicky, this is Beast. Beast, this is my little sidekick."

"Ah, pleased to meet you. But please, call me Alfonse. So, you're the one Arthur's been telling me about. The changeling."

"Changeling?" Vicky tugged at her ponytail, eyes darting around the space.

"Oh, sorry, showing my age there. The lycanthrope? Werewolf?"

"Um, yes, that's me." Vicky pouted then stuck out her chest; her reputation had gone to her head.

Many of the shifters in the city now treated her with respect bordering on worship, and she loved it. Everyone in the community had heard what had gone down, about our escapade up north, and how wild she was. They didn't know about Ivan though, or their relationship, and both wanted it kept that way.

Still, she'd become almost insufferable at times, and needed to watch herself or she'd end up in a lot of trouble. You know, more trouble than usual.

"So," said Alfonse, once upon a time only ever known as Beast, although he was still that now if you went by looks alone. "You come to get buff?"

"You know it," I replied with a smile.

Alfonse grunted as he picked up a thick steel bar I couldn't wrap my hands around, with a series of monstrous cogs slotted on so it became a makeshift barbell, just one that weighed more than a mere mortal could ever hope to lift let alone curl, and banged out a quick set of curls. His biceps almost popped through his tight skin as blood surged into the muscles. Vicky and I watched, mesmerized.

He paused after his set, smiled, then knocked out another set. This must be his warm-up.

The room was large, another old cistern, and it was crammed with all manner of strange homemade machines and some commercial equipment plus a lot of bits and pieces he'd picked up from car boot sales or scrap yards. He preferred the homemade stuff as any commercial gear simply wasn't heavy enough, so he fashioned bars and machines of all description from whatever he could get his hands on that weighed a shit-load, the end result being a room full of pulleys and chains and cogs and wheels connected to lots of very heavy stuff.

His relaxation zone consisted of padded benches he'd made so they'd take his weight, the only nod to current seating trends a large sofa he'd assembled without much modifying, the wonders of Scandinavian ingenuity, that faced a large coffee table full of muscle mags and a huge TV.

Basically it was like a gym for giants, or trolls maybe, and he was definitely capable of eating goats, and apparently when he was younger did exactly that.

"Who are you?" asked Vicky as she took in the gym-cum-lair.

"He's the Beast," I said with pride as I tried to pick up a dumbbell made from two thick cogs welded to a section of scaffold bar. I couldn't get the damn thing off the ground.

"That was a long time ago. I'm just Alfonse."

"But... but you're huge. I mean really huge."

"I think he knows that," I said.

"What, this frail body?" asked Alfonse as he flexed a bicep. "Been getting small lately, need to eat more."

"Um, if you say so."

"Right, that's enough chit-chat, we came here to work out," I said, stripping down to combats and white vest.

Vicky did a double-take from me to Alfonse and back again, and I suddenly felt self-conscious. I'd always been wiry, but tried to keep in shape. I got bored of jogging though, although I kept it up so I always had stamina to run from the bad guys, but had begun coming to see Alfonse three times a week if I possibly could to have a real workout. It helped with the insomnia for a few hours each night that I punished my body. Not perfect, but better than nothing.

"What? Stop looking at me like that. You can't compare me to him, he's been working out for hundreds of years and it's all genetics anyway."

"No, um, I know he's bigger, like a lot bigger, but you're looking pretty good." Vicky scanned up and down my beastly body, the patchy hair, the skin riddled with scar tissue, the veins and what little muscle I thought I had, but she seemed genuinely impressed.

"I told you, Arthur, you are looking impressive. For a twig anyway. Haha."

"You guys mean it? Really?"

Alfonse nodded and Vicky took an unconscious step forward, her hand reaching out. She caught herself and lowered it, but said, "Yeah, you look good. Especially for an old guy."

"Hey, I'm the same age as you, but thanks."

"Don't remind me."

"Okay, let's get this session started," I said, feeling damn pleased with myself, even though I was, of course, over such vanity and couldn't care less if someone thought I looked good or not.

For the next two hours we were put through a series of grueling, painful rituals involving pulleys and weights and benches designed for torture. We were made to perform a myriad of exercises on countless machines, with Alfonse, all three hundred and fifty pounds of him, and it was all muscle, bellowing at us in his beautiful, but nonetheless intimidating voice, to do one more rep and to "Hold it, hold it," and "Squeeze," and "Let it burn," and other esoteric bro-speak that held little meaning beyond that we had to keep going or get shouted at some more.

Finally spent, lying exhausted and drenched in sweat on the concrete floor, I gasped for air as Vicky panted like a knackered greyhound beside me. We turned to face each other, and smiled.

"Now, that's what I call a workout," I said.

Vicky rolled over and puked.

I laughed. Or maybe cackled.

Time to Feast

Half an hour later, as Beast grunted and clanged weights about, what he called just getting a bit of a pump, Vicky and I finally rolled over and helped each other up. We were still soaked in sweat, still panting, and every muscle in my body ached. I was also walking like a constipated duck.

"That was great, eh?" I said, grinning in what I knew was a rather manic manner, the endorphins rushing through my bloodstream giving me a high almost as good as magic.

"Ugh, I think I'm going to throw up again." Vicky doubled over, and sure enough, she did.

"See, I told you those aerobics in front of the TV were a waste of time."

Vicky wiped her face on a sweaty towel and snapped, "Shut up."

"Hey, just trying to help. Keep you in shape."

Fact was, I had an ulterior motive apart from wanting us both to get some sleep this night before the handover in the morning. I was hoping I'd get her appetite going and she'd finally eat. Ever since the whole "Whoa, you're a wolf," thing, she'd lost even more weight, and although she was still shapely I knew all the warning signs, had seen them many times over the years. She was stressed whether she'd admit it or not. Who could blame her? But her eating disorder was always the first thing to get out of hand.

Alfonse untangled himself from a torture device he said helped build his lats, lats apparently being the big bit of your back, although someone must have stolen mine, and thudded over.

"Same time Wednesday?" he asked.

"You can count on it," I gasped, studying the big guy again.

"You're nuts, both of you," Vicky whispered, her throat hoarse.

"You not gonna make it, little lady?" he asked.

"I'm busy."

"Doing what?" I asked.

"Anything."

I gave Alfonse a bro hug, Vicky kind of patted him on the back, or at least a massive lump of meat that was part of his back, and we left to the grunts and the clangs deep beneath the streets of our city.

We dragged our aching legs back the way we'd come, both doing good impressions of arthritic penguins, which may or may not have been an improvement on the duck shuffle. At the exit point, I shoved on Vicky's bony, quivering ass—she'd developed a tic and her cheeks wobbled like electrocuted jelly—to get her up the ladder, then I clambered up with muscles screaming and legs shaking and cramping, dropped the lid that felt like it weighed a million and one pounds back into place, and we waddled, moaned, and spasmed off into the night.

Vicky trailed behind, bitching about sore bits she didn't even know were actual bits until now, so I turned and asked, "You wanna grab a bite? I know a place."

"Around here?" she asked dubiously.

"Yeah. Don't worry, nothing will happen to us."

Vicky shrugged, then her stomach rumbled.

Deeper into the wasteland of urban detritus, where there were no vehicles, no passersby, no rumble of traffic above, no nothing but concrete and garbage, we entered a small shantytown, a collection of tarps and scrap the occupants scavenged to shelter from the weather.

"What are we doing here?" whispered Vicky, eyes scanning around constantly.

"Getting something to eat. Trust me, it'll be worth it." I took her arm, led her aside, then pulled back a tatty sheet.

Inside was warm, the cramped, low-ceilinged interior lit by a large fire in a repurposed feed trough behind a makeshift counter. Cheap, smoky candles were dotted about at upended empty cable reels used as tables. Most were taken. It was little more than a shed really, albeit a big one, but the smell, oh if only I could describe it to you. Juicy steaks cooked however you wanted them, a mug of coffee or tea, and even a piece of lettuce if you were health-conscious.

Behind the plank of smooth wood that acted as a counter, Archer was busy watching over sizzling, spitting steaks with a keen eye. And I mean just the one. He bobbed his head ten times, then flipped them off onto plates, spun and dropped them onto the counter, and two guys wrapped up tight against any weather the UK could throw at them grabbed them hungrily and said thank you.

Archer grunted, then his attention drifted to us. He nodded.

"Hey, Archer. Busy tonight?"

Archer nodded. He liked to nod. And cook. It was his thing. Nodding and cooking. He liked being moody too.

"How'd you like yours? I asked Vicky.

"What?"

"Steak, dummy. How do you want it?"

"Um, er, well done, please."

"Make mine medium." I put down four notes on the counter. Archer raised an eyebrow, and I said, "Been a good week." He nodded thanks then began cooking.

We took a table, and by that I mean we squeezed past the hungry and the homeless or the merely cold, and sat on the freshly swept floor covered in cardboard, changed daily.

Vicky looked around dubiously and her nose twitched up in a very condescending way.

Keeping my voice low, I said, "Don't worry, it's clean, it's safe, and it's helping."

"Helping who?"

"Archer. He's a great chef, and he only charges if you have the money, so if you have any you give what you can, and it gives everyone somewhere they can fall back on. He won't stand for trouble, and you don't want to make him angry, but this is where I like to eat sometimes. Especially after a workout with Beast."

I guess Vicky was used to me taking her to odd places by now. I knew the city in different ways to her, knew different people, all part of the job, this underground, gangster life I had chosen for myself. So she didn't push, ask why Archer didn't speak, ask why people lived like this, as she knew from her experience with me that this was life for some people, that not everyone could cope with bills and be a citizen. Some people had issues, or merely chose a different path.

But she did ask about Beast.

"Does Alfonse live down there?"

"Sure does."

"Why? And how is he that big? Does he work out all day? Is he a steroid abuser?"

"Haha, Vicky, you poor innocent thing. No, he doesn't do steroids. Yes, he works out almost non-stop, and eats like you wouldn't believe, hence the wall of fridges and freezers, but he comes up and goes shopping, does other normal stuff. Apparently he's even got a car, but he likes it down there, has lived that way for years, decades actually. He's kind of old-fashioned, gave up the wizarding and the gangster life, mostly, before I was born."

"He's a wizard!?"

"Sure is. Or was. Not all of us have beards and look like someone scrunched up our face. Some wizards, er, they do things differently, find their own way."

"But why?"

"Why? Because he likes to lift heavy stuff. It's his hobby. It beats dealing with clients and getting chased around by goons. It's his thing."

The steaks arrived, looking delicious, smelling even better, and as I tucked in with gusto, Vicky took a tentative bite, smiled, and then wolfed it down. No pun intended.

Ten minutes later we were out the door, okay, sheet, and soon enough we were back in the car.

"Fancy a milkshake?" I asked.

Her eyes slits, Vicky vibed me, trying to do her gangster-mom stare, then said, "Are you winding me up? I think I've had enough for one night."

"Me too," I said with a smile. "I'm beat. I'm going to sleep a few hours tonight, I can feel it."

"So am I."

There was a rap at the window and I turned in time to see Nathan, the goddamn posh twat of a broker, and the face of Cerberus, I no longer cared to broker with, smile his smug smile as he lifted his cane.

I knew it was no normal walking aid, that he used it to help with his dodgy leg but also it was a staff of magic, so I shoved Vicky's head down, rolled out of the car, and readied to blast.

The evening had gone so well, too.

Nathan

"I want to show you something."

"Fuck off. No, actually, stay right there so I can kill you. You've screwed with me one time too many, Nathan. You promised to leave me alone but your goons almost killed us yesterday. Um, or was it the day before?" I asked Vicky.

Acting like it was an invitation to get out, she clambered across the seats then exited and stood beside me, hands on hips. The effect was somewhat spoiled as she had to stand on tip-toe to see over the car door. "Yesterday. Although it was before dawn so maybe that counts as the day before." Vicky scratched her pert nose and tried to glare at Nathan. He smiled back at her like she was a cute puppy dog.

"Whatever. I'm going to kill you anyway."

"Arthur, if you would give me a minute to explain before you try to kill me?" Nathan smoothed his sandy hair, in that annoying, languid, posh way I can't describe but just screams, "I'm a posh bugger and very confident and look, I wear tweed suits whatever the weather." He winced a little as the cane took less weight then adjusted his position. I kept one eye on him, one on the cane. I knew he could do rudimentary magic, just nothing in my league. But never underestimate a posh twat in tweed if they know magic, if for no other reason than their smug face as they get the better of you will haunt you until your dying day.

"Why should I? And how did you find me?" I asked, glaring at him, feeling the power stir inside.

"You should know I have many means by now. And why should you trust me? Because I had nothing to do with what happened this time. Things are, er, changing, and my superiors are becoming antsy. They want you gone, out of the picture. Say you're a liability."

"Because I keep taking things they want for themselves. You want to keep these items away from us, but it isn't your place. Ugh, I can't be bothered with this, we've had this conversation a thousand times. Just stand still so I can kill you. It'll hurt. Promise."

I swear I was so close to doing it, seconds away, and I really wish I'd just killed him and had done with it. I didn't trust him, liked him about as much as I liked sprouts, and wanted to wipe that smug smile off his slender, handsome face once and for all.

"I want to show you something. It might change your mind, make you think twice about the artifacts you take. About who you give them to."

"Look, Nathan, I'm careful about who I take from and who I give to. People have a right to these things, it helps them. You just lock them away and refuse to let them be used, be read, whatever the case may be."

"As you say, we have been over this many times. So let me show you something. If you want to kill me after, then you can try. What have you got to lose?"

"My life, or several hours of it at least. And I don't like the company."

"Can I come?" asked Vicky, eyes sparkling as she imagined who knew what.

"My dear lady, of course you can. You are Arthur's partner, after all. In fact, I insist."

"Sidekick, that's what she is. She's the comic relief." I glared at Vicky. "Although she's failing miserably at that lately."

"Am not. Er, the comic relief. And I'm funny if I want to be." Vicky stomped her foot and splashed muddy water all over her leggings. I just raised an eyebrow and waited for her to say something. She didn't.

"Give me one good reason why I should come with you, trust you? It's probably a trap."

"I give you my word as a gentleman, as an equal. I swear on Cerberus and all I hold dear that I will not try to harm you. I want you on my side, I want you on our side. This is my last chance, my last hope. After this it's out of my hands I'm afraid. Moving forward, if this fails, our dealings will not be pleasant."

"Being ousted, are you"? I wondered what was happening, if he was being removed from his position as the second most important figure in Cerberus—the leader was a mystery man I knew nothing about. Maybe Nathan was in trouble for not stopping me, or maybe there was the usual political crap going on and this was a minor issue. I didn't kid myself I was that important. Just good at my job. Very good.

"My actions, and motives, are being questioned, doubted even, but I told them you aren't easy to kill, and now we are down several Hounds because of their faith in me. My superior isn't pleased. He gets annoyed about such things."

"Whatever. Fine, let's go, but no funny business," I warned.

"Wouldn't dream of it, my dear fellow."

I refrained from smacking Nathan into next week, but it was hard. Who the hell speaks like that? It was like he was born in another world, which, I guess, he was. I did not have a privileged upbringing, no silver spoon in my mouth.

Nathan pulled out a phone, spoke a few words, and five minutes later, after a very awkward silence, a helicopter landed.

"Cool," squealed Vicky.

"Bugger," I moaned.

A Sickness

I'm not good with helicopters, or anything small hurtling through the air. It ain't right, not natural. If I was meant to fly, I'd have wings. And I don't. At least not the last time I checked.

"You okay, Arthur?" Nathan asked with mock concern, his lip twitching as his smirk spread.

"You look green. Actually green," yelled Vicky, her face flushed with excitement as she leaned close to the door.

"I'm... fine." I wasn't.

Nathan communicated with the pilot via a headset on his helmet, but I couldn't hear what they were saying and didn't want to. I just wanted this to be over.

Nathan shifted in his seat and I turned to watch him to take my mind off things. His smirk was gone, replaced with a frown. He leaned forward a little and said something short and sharp, and the pilot turned and nodded seriously. He didn't look happy.

Then a single feather fell, from inside the freaking helicopter. I put out my hand and everyone watched as it drifted slowly into my palm.

It was black. I'd seen it before. I got a bad feeling.

Like sound being sucked out of the world, the engine died and the blades stopped whirring. I knew enough about helicopters to know that wasn't good, and then my stomach made a dash for my mouth as we plummeted over the capital of the UK, which I knew definitely wasn't good.

"This is why I hate flying," I muttered as I looked for the parachutes. But this was a helicopter, and apparently they fly so low you don't have a chance to use one before you get squashed. Which to my mind was an excellent reason why they should be banned. Or used to punish people, something like that.

We carried on falling. Or crashing, or plummeting, whatever you call it when you drop out of the sky in something that by rights shouldn't be able to fly in the first place.

Up It Comes

"It's mine," came a whisper from inside the helicopter.

Everyone turned to each other, unsure who had spoken. But I knew it wasn't anyone physically present.

"Return what you stole."

"Um, what was it?" I asked, surprising myself with how cool I was. Guess me and Death had a long history and I wasn't as worried as the others were.

"You know."

"Actually, no, there's been quite a few things I've taken. Can you narrow it down?"

"Arthur!" shouted Nathan. "Stop messing about." He gripped the seat hard, veins throbbing. Vicky was praying.

"Shut up, everyone, I'm handling this." Black feathers fell like snow, and the interior was frosty. The glass began to ice up and my teeth started to chatter.

"What you took this night belongs to me. I want it."

"Okay, but if I die you get nothing," I said, wondering how long it took for a helicopter to crash. Judging by how close the ground looked, not long at all. Just time enough to piss off a disembodied entity.

There was no reply, just a terrifying roar as the engine kicked in. The rotors whoop, whooped, began to spin fast, and we flipped to the side as the pilot struggled with the controls.

"I told you," shouted Nathan. "I told you repeatedly that you should stop, but you won't listen."

"Shut up. Whoever that was, if you'd taken what he wanted then he'd be after you instead. I stand by my principles, and that is I steal things and get paid. It's always gonna piss somebody off."

"Or something," whispered Vicky.

"Hey, Vicky, looking a bit green there." I gave her a wink, that'd teach her to make fun of me.

My humor vanished as Vicky puked up over my boots. It returned when she put a hand to her mouth and sprayed Nathan head-to-toe with chunks of quality steak. What a waste. Worth it though to see Nathan's face.

The helicopter righted, I picked black feathers off my trousers, and the pilot landed, turned off the engines, and generally fiddled about with switches and levers that looked impossibly complicated. As the blades slowed, I had a minor heart attack but kept it to myself.

I could hear Death cackling from behind the veil, saying, "Oh, so close, Arthur, you jammy git."

"You're telling me," I grumbled.

"What?" asked Vicky, wiping her mouth.

"Nothing, just talking to an old friend."

Haha

Nathan wiped himself down with handkerchiefs and wet wipes and dropped them all into a bag he left in the helicopter.

"Follow me," he said with a glare at Vicky.

"You don't want to ask about the spooky voice in the helicopter? Comment on the fact we almost died?"

"Why?" he snapped. "You know who it was, what it was?"

"Maybe I do, maybe I don't," I replied, scratching at my beard, then wobbling. I lost focus for a moment and began to teeter, but snapped back to reality even as sleep called me. My muscles were cramping up. I needed electrolytes, or maybe electrocuting, something to jolt me to my senses. "Can we do this another day? I'm sleepy." I swear I could have stretched out and gone to sleep on the damn helipad.

"You can sleep later, this is important. And we won't get another chance. As I told you, there is turmoil within our organization, so this may be your last chance to see."

"See what?" I was honestly past caring by now, but whatever, it was worth a shot.

"All in good time, dear boy."

"I swear, if you call me that one more time... Ugh, fuck it, just hurry up."

"And I have to get home," said Vicky. "My girls need me."

"Yeah, Nathan, and the Slug, er, her husband needs her too. Do you have a family? Any kids dressed in tweed diapers with silver spoons hanging out their mouths?"

"Arthur, don't push me. I'm trying here, but you don't make it easy." With that, Nathan strode across a lawn so perfect it was like a bowling green and toward a door in the quadrant. I swear, it was like being in Hogwarts or something, all Oxford University style with a gothic twist. Proper posh place, not my scene at all.

I shrugged at Vicky, wondered if my brain was giving out from lack of sleep, and we followed.

I was definitely losing my edge. I'd missed another chance to kill him and save us a lot of grief.

The Warehouse

We entered through a discreet wooden door, the carved arch above finely detailed just like the rest of the building. It led directly into a long hallway with dark oak flooring, paneled walls, and downlit paintings of old dudes in robes, looking pompous. Exactly what you'd expect from a posh government spook building full of old-timers playing their games.

As far as I knew, Nathan was very high up in some kind of secret service type organization and this was the headquarters, somewhere we'd followed him to and spied from the front entrance, but precisely what the organization was, and his exact position, Vicky, even with her mad skills, failed to discover.

But what was more important was that it was definitely a front for Cerberus, and maybe they were both inextricably tied, that one went hand in hand with the other. Cerberus had, for centuries, taken it upon themselves to try to gather all magical artifacts and would do anything to accomplish that, including duping me for years into helping them, something that still smarts to this day.

Their Hounds were soulless, robotic goons who would do whatever it took to get what they wanted, including trying to kill me on numerous occasions, with Nathan often taking the lead. We'd finally come to an understanding, meaning, if they all stayed out of my way I wouldn't kill Nathan, but I really, really wanted to. I'd been certain he was behind this latest interruption to my business, but now he was saying he wasn't, and he was about to show me something he believed would what, make me side with him and his nutters? Help him keep his job?

Guess I'd find out.

We walked down endless pristine corridors, each as understated as the last, but somehow managing to still scream money and tradition, exclusiveness and secrecy. Men in cramped rooms full of books and rich furnishings stared at us uneasily as we passed, aides carrying mounds of paperwork hurried past, nodding politely to Nathan and staring at Vicky and me with suspicion. Through a series of doors and richly carpeted stairwells with oak banisters, we descended to more sterile corridors, where the doors were all closed and the aides looked more like goons. We got increasingly suspicious glances, and Nathan had to stop more often to talk to goons, but nobody stopped us.

Then we traveled via several elevators operated by a key card, deeper and deeper under the city, until we emerged in what appeared to be the service level. We walked down a long stretch of corridor where ducts, pipes, and bunches of color-coded cables fought for space on the walls and ceiling. The only sound was the hum of the heating system and the tap-tap-tapping of Nathan's cane. None of us had spoken a word to each other the whole time, but I could sense where we were heading, knew where he was taking us.

As we walked, the pressure built in the corridor until it became almost overwhelming. This was nothing to do with the building itself, no lessening of air quality or failure of the building's systems, these were magical whispers. Tiny, infinitesimal leaks compounded until they formed an almost physical barrier, and certainly a mental one. Wherever we were headed, it was barely contained, and what was leaking was enough to cause serious disruption if it wasn't carefully monitored.

Vicky stumbled and I grabbed her arm.

"You okay?"

"Just felt a bit funny," she said, not looking well.

"Nathan, is this safe? I assume you can feel it too?"

Nathan turned, but didn't stop moving. "No, it isn't safe, and yes, I can feel it. We should be fine, it's been like this for a long time. Don't worry, once we're inside there are, ah, devices at work to lessen the effects."

"Inside what?" asked Vicky as I held on to her and we caught up with Nathan.

"Inside the warehouse," said Nathan, spreading his arms wide, being overly dramatic if you ask me.

Soon enough we reached the end of the corridor, and rather than turning and continuing on our way, he stopped at a door just like all the others.

"This it?" I asked, knowing it was. Reality itself felt wrong here, just off enough to make my hat vibrate and my wand tingle in my pocket.

Nathan nodded. "It is."

"Are you sure about this? I don't know what your game is, but whatever you show me, it won't make us buddies."

"Just let me do this. I'm all out of ideas otherwise. This is important, Arthur."

"Whatever."

We stood back while Nathan used his key card and the door opened after several clunks of what sounded like bolts withdrawing. It was no normal door, it looked like it was straight out of a bank vault. One that housed priceless goodies.

"Oh, great, another boring fucking corridor."

"If you please?" Nathan entered then swept his hand forward, inviting us in.

We glanced at each other, then, me still holding on to Vicky, we entered. The door slammed closed behind us, the corridor hummed into life, and I felt reality turn back to normal as the magical emanations lifted.

"It's a scrubbing room, state-of-the-art," said Nathan, as the sound in the corridor increased, a whooshing noise like it was sucking the magic right out of the air.

"Never heard of magical scrubbers," I said.

"Me either," said Vicky. "They don't exist or I'd know about them."

"There's much you don't know. Cerberus is no amateur outfit. We have resources. We have people, smart people."

"So why'd they put you in charge?" I asked, smiling.

"Haha, very funny. Now, shall we enter? Are you ready?"

We nodded, and followed Nathan to another door at the end of the short corridor, the lights getting brighter as we passed, like out of some sci-fi movie.

Again, the key card was used, yet when the door opened it was to utter darkness. "Follow me. Take a few steps and wait for the door to close.

I had a bad feeling, but then, I usually did. Nonetheless, we followed him, and stood in the darkness as the door closed with a clunk.

Light erupted from high above, easily three stories, blinding me for a moment. I looked down to find we were standing on a metal gantry with a railing several paces away, and then, and then...

"Well, fuck me sideways," said Vicky.

We stared at her in shock, but I understood, as I was now looking where she was looking, and I said, "Yeah, me too," and even whistled. It was one of those moments.

Lots of Stuff

"Is this what I think it is?" I asked Nathan, somehow managing to get the words out when all I wanted to do was gawp. My anger was rising, and fast, but I held myself in check as this was too important, too momentous, to screw things up right now. I was sure I'd manage that later.

"If what you think it is is a vast warehouse full of dangerous magical items Cerberus have collected over centuries then yes, it is."

"What a waste," I lamented, looking down on row after row of industrial racking containing shelves full of locked metal crates of varying sizes.

"It stops people like you causing havoc in the world," said Nathan, actually serious.

"Bullshit, pure bullshit. I get it, okay? That you think keeping all this stuff locked up is for the greater good, stops wizards and practitioners blowing up the world or something, but that's not reality."

"Oh, enlighten me."

"Fine, I will. Most items go to collectors, and they look after them. Others are used to aid with magic, to help us, but, again, they are guarded closely. Why'd you think there are people like me? Because it's fucking hard to get these things. But I'll tell you one thing, Nathan, and about this I am utterly correct. What we all know, what wizards, warlocks, even the lowest bloody student knows, is that you don't, because it would be fucking stupid bordering on suicidal, like inviting Armageddon... Ugh, Buster's hat, where do I start? Okay," I sighed and took a deep breath, how could Cerberus be this monumentally stupid? "What you don't bloody do is put thousands of insanely powerful, unknowable magical items in one place."

"I'd never thought about that," said Vicky, eyes glued to the boxes. How big was this place? I couldn't see the end.

"Well I have, ever since I took up this line of work. It's best if things constantly change hands, so the items don't get too comfortable and the owners too lax. When people pay a ton of money for something, they look after it, protect it. They cherish and guard it. They may use it, sure, but mostly it's books, small things to help with spells and the like. Some have maybe a dozen or more items, and you can feel the power simmering when you get anywhere near to a collection like that. Hell knows what kind of power this lot is giving off. I've told you from the start, it's a ridiculous thing you guys do. You have no right to decide who gets to have what, and storing it like this is the worst thing you could possibly do. It's safer in the hands of many individuals. And besides, it's magic, it should be shared."

"Arthur, that's quite a speech, and I agree." Nathan turned from looking at the warehouse and faced me.

"Oh! Yeah, right. So, um, what's all this about then?"

"Isn't it obvious?"

"No, it isn't." I got a very bad feeling, and I cursed my loving, trusting nature.

"I want what you took, this night. What that, ah, creature wanted back. What you're delivering to the vampires in a few hours. I want it. It's the key to controlling this, all of it."

"You double-crossing piece of shit!" Magic built inside of me, welling up as my will forced it to power-up like I was a robot superhero. I pulled open the Velcro and delved into my pocket for my wand. "This is the last time you screw with me, Nathan."

Nathan smiled his infuriating smile, lifted his cane, and waved it about in admonishment. "No need to get angry. I knew you couldn't resist something like this. But you must understand, Arthur, I have no choice. My people really are up against it, and my position really is in jeopardy. And we do need to think about moving some of our inventory, but I am in trouble, because you're still alive, and interfering. You have to be stopped. I am going to stop you. After you hand over what you took. You don't know what it is, do you?"

"So what if I don't? I did a job, I trust Ivan, weird as that sounds, and besides, Vicky wants to build an extension. Prepare to die, mother—"

I yanked my wand out and forced my will deep into it, waiting for sigils to flare and energy to incinerate his goddamn head. Nothing happened. I stared down at the cold length of wood in my hand, and then dropped my arm.

"Shit!"

"What? What's wrong?" screeched Vicky. "Blast him. Let's get out of here."

"It's the scrubbers, right?" I asked Nathan, feeling like a first-class dick.

"Exactly." And then he smiled that smug smile of his and I kind of lost it.

"Guess what, Nathan, my dear boy?"

His smile wavered and he asked cautiously, "What?"

"I've been working out." And with that I just ran forward, shoved him hard, and he flew backward and careened against the railing.

I stepped back out of arm's reach, and readied for a fight, but Nathan was smart, and sneaky, so he lunged forward for Vicky.

Shocked, Vicky scrammed at his eyes as he grabbed her arm and he released her, staggering back. Wild, Vicky screamed at him, "Don't touch me!" and pushed him. Hard.

Nathan teetered for a moment, almost recovered his balance, then his bad leg gave way. He slipped, fell backward hard against the railing again, and flipped over. He even made it look professional, like a diver showing off a new move.

There was a loud thud moments later and I couldn't help but be shocked by it. Had it finally happened? Was I finally rid of what I guess you could call my arch-enemy?

We moved to the railing and stared down.

Nathan's body lay at an impossible angle, his skull was split wide open, brain and blood was spreading on the concrete floor.

"Yup, he's dead all right. Let's go."

We spun as the door opened; things took a turn for the worse.

Panic

Something crackled in the dark corridor, the lights extinguished, blue lightning forked and it was as though the blackness itself shot out at us. It hit me right in the guts and I slammed back against the railing. All I could think was that it would be ironic if I met the same fate as Nathan. I wouldn't let it happen, if for no other reason than I couldn't bear to see his smug face after I died, as he'd be sure to be having a nice cup of tea with Death just so he could ridicule me.

With a grunt, I lifted my wand, then remembered the damn scrubbers and instead rushed forward, grabbing Vicky by the arm as I passed her.

Blackness whirled around in frenzied spirals of malevolent fury, a shriek of rage grinding like a chainsaw in my head.

And then it stopped, just stopped, and the lights in the corridor blinked back on with a buzz, my head cleared, and I understood that the scrubbers in the warehouse were so strong that they'd stopped this thing dead in its tracks, its energy negated.

For how long, and how effectively, I didn't wait to find out. This was tied up with the helicopter attack, and Nathan had known what it was, but he was history, and good riddance.

Never mind, The Hat would investigate, but he needed to get the hell out of here first. He also needed his sleep, and he definitely needed a fucking word with the vampires for getting him into this nonsense.

First, he needed to stay alive.

"Let's go," I said calmly to Vicky as I pulled her into the corridor. As is the way with these things, the lights flickered then went out again.

The warehouse door slammed shut, leaving us in pitch black. Vicky moaned, but I didn't stop, just sped up until we were running.

"Arthur, stop it, you're going to get us killed. We'll smash into the door," Vicky wailed.

"Not if I have anything to do with it."

Taking advantage of the scrubbers being out of action, and with the magical backlash of the artifacts pounding at my head, and a furious, maleficent creature hammering at my back in rage and frustration, I lifted my wand, shunted my will, my frustration, and my need for self-preservation down into it and grinned manically as the sigils flared into life, lighting the way.

Vicky gasped, and my smile turned to a frown as the door, closed and very solid, was highlighted right in front of us.

I whispered a spell under my breath, something I do when nervous although spells have no power without the intent and power of the speaker. A fat plate of fierce red heat spat from the wand and slammed into the steel, melting it in an instant.

We dove through, landing hard and painfully out in the boring corridor. Vicky rolled off me, sprang to her feet, and I reached back through the hole in the door, still hissing around the edges, grabbed my hat, put Grace back where she belonged, pushed off with my feet and sprinted after the already running Vicky.

Black feathers drifted down in front of us as we ran, then were gone. We were alone in the depths of Cerberus HQ.

I didn't have a clue how to get out. "Should have taken Nathan's key card," I muttered as we kept on running.

Vicky to the Rescue

"Don't worry about that, you've got me." Vicky's ponytail bobbed about like a happy dog's tail as she tried to keep up with my long stride. It's not that I am particularly tall, it's just that she was like a miniature poodle. Or something else that's small and annoying.

"Oh, yeah, whoopee." I tried to think about how to escape, but I'd seen no stairwells this deep down, and assumed they'd have locks too.

"Just get us to the elevator, I'll get us in." Vicky's face was set in grim determination, so I focused on retracing our steps and got us there in record time. Meaning, we only got lost twice.

How long before alarms began ringing? How long before that thing reappeared? How long before I fell asleep, or went into a coma?

"Okay, we're here. What now?"

"Now I do what I do best." Vicky fished about in her rucksack, some designer nonsense made mostly of straps, the actual bag so small it looked pretty much pointless, an afterthought to the fashion designer but a perfect place to emblazon the logo.

"What, annoy me and ask for money?"

"No, tech stuff, you twat."

"Hey, I'm the one that says twat. I'm the boss." There was a long pause as Vicky stared at me. "Twat," I said, and we both laughed. Okay, I did. She just punched me on the arm then dragged what looked like a very sleek modern phone and a load of wires out of her twat-bag. Um, er, that came out wrong. Sorry.

"Waddya doing?" I asked as she tapped on the screen and fiddled with wires.

"Don't worry about it, you wouldn't understand."

"Try me."

"Okay," she said as she worked. "I'm going to bypass the blah, blah, blah, blah, and see if I can port a blah, blah, blah, and if that works I can access the blah, and blah it and then the blah should allow me to blah, blah, blah, blah, blah, and then I can use that to blah and—"

Ping.

The door opened and Vicky lifted up a hand to high-five.

"Just get in, we haven't got time for that." Vicky looked crestfallen. "Haha, just kidding. Good job." We high-fived and Vicky hopped in as the door closed.

"You were doing that thing again, weren't you?"

"Don't know what you mean," I said innocently, raising my eyes to stare at the ceiling.

"Liar. You zoned out the minute I started explaining."

"Did not."

"Okay, what did I say then?"

"Something about the ports and the arrays and bypassing the doobies to gain access to the frazzles and then you could gee up the monkeys and make them triangulate the numerical outliers of space. That right?"

"Dick." Vicky hit me again. But this time she did smile.

Yeah, The Hat still had it. Never lost it.

Ping.

The door opened, and we stepped out, all casual like, blending in perfectly amongst the suits and the business skirts, and we didn't walk fast or end up running or anything. And we didn't have loads of people shouting at us and alarms didn't begin to ring as we crashed through the door from earlier into the inner courtyard and run into the center where we could then be spied on from every angle.

We might have done something similar though, but with style, obviously.

"What now?" asked Vicky, out of breath, sweating like a Pygmy in discount sportswear.

"Can you fly a helicopter?"

"No, can you?"

"Well, now that you ask," I said, and her face lit up. "No. But how hard can it be?"

We jumped in, and sat in the front seats.

I couldn't even find the key to start it. Did they have keys, or was it just buttons?

"What's the backup plan?" asked Vicky, pressing random buttons same as me.

"Backup plan? I didn't even have a main plan. Um, how about... No, that won't work." I glanced out the window and said, "Ah, how about we keep on running?"

Vicky spied the goons charging across the grass and shrieked.

"Hello? Faery godmother?" I called. "You know that thing about coming in the nick of time to save me, and how you never do? Well, maybe just this once you could?" I asked sweetly into the air. I waited for the faery dust to start falling, but it didn't.

What did fall was a single black feather, and it landed on my nose.

We were screwed.

Doing It In Style

Men rushed toward us, my nose tickled, Vicky jabbed her fingers at anything she could, and I searched the interior frantically, sure there must be an easy way to get the damn thing started.

"Start," I muttered, pointing my wand at the array of mystical buttons and switches. White energy crackled from the tip of my wand in a panic that was clearly contagious and the helicopter juddered then spasmed into life.

The blades spun and over the roar I shouted to Vicky, "Strap in," as I yanked on the harness as fast as I could.

Vicky's eyes widened but she managed to get herself secured even as she shouted, "Is this a good idea?"

"No, a very bad one," I bellowed as a goon yanked the door open and I kicked him squarely in the head.

How did I get it off the ground? More buttons, or just pull back on one of the levers? There was one to my left, one in front of me between my legs, but there were also pedals. Did it work like a manual car? Were there gears?

"Ah, fuck it," I groaned, and pulled back on the lever to the left, or was it the other one? I was so panicked I honestly didn't know what I was doing. The deathtrap rose with a terrible whining that I was sure wasn't good, but at least we were off the ground, which was good. What was definitely not good were the men fanned out beneath us, all carrying weapons, all pointing up at us.

I cackled as we lifted higher, no way would they shoot. We'd crash and probably explode and their precious building would go up in flames. I settled into my seat, turned and winked at Vicky, who, for some reason, was sweating and gripping the seat so tight she was pulling out the stuffing. Then I focused on my flying.

We were above the top of the building now but all we'd done was go up, we had to actually get away. Which way? Like it mattered. I carefully grabbed the controls between my legs and gave an experimental jiggle. Bad move, the helicopter shuddered and wobbled like we were gonna flip, so I put it back into its center position and we leveled off.

Vicky looked at me dubiously, I shrugged my shoulders, and tried again. Gently. We angled to the left and banked that way, but lost altitude almost immediately. Hell, how complicated could they make these things? So I had to control the lift and the angle, how was that supposed to work? And what about the pedals?

I wiggled things, I pressed down on things I ought not to press down on, and I used what I guess was like a steering wheel to turn us in several directions until I saw somewhere we could land and make our escape.

Then I took a breath, blew the feathers from my face, and went for it.

As we increased speed and banked hard to the right, we shot over the tops of the buildings and past the heaving, morose traffic, through air thick with noxious chemicals toward trees and fields. Even metropolises such as this have parks; you have to keep the populace at least semi-sane if they are to remain.

The ride was not thrilling, the ride was not smooth, the ride was mostly a hardly controlled hurtle toward a very uncertain future as I tried to control the speed, and failed miserably as how the hell were you supposed to think about, let alone operate, two things at once? Apparently, women can do it, or they say they can. I believe it. Inevitably, we turned left sharply and clipped the trees. That was it, we were out of control, just a few minutes from Cerberus HQ.

Thinking it best to let gravity do what it did best, and having watched enough movies to know that a crashing helicopter with spinning blades was never a good idea, I flashed weak magic at the controls and they sparked then the motor died.

As we spun and headed nose-first toward a playing field, thankfully empty at such an ungodly hour apart from several dog walkers, the world suddenly became silent as the rotors slowed without power. With no time to think about the consequences of my next move, I released my harness, reached over Vicky and did the same to hers, grabbed her in a tight bear hug, blasted her door away, and pushed off hard with my feet.

We fell from on high like two battered bricks tied with a piece of string, the helicopter made a weird cranking noise—you probably aren't meant to shut them down mid-flight—then plummeted into the park and exploded in a most spectacular way. The resulting shockwave lifted us from our descent and shunted us sideways, slamming us into a tree that would have crushed our bones and our stupid heads if I hadn't put up a hurried, and not quite perfect protective shield that bounced us off a branch. We careened backward, hit the trunk of another tree that took the air out of me, and then we smacked into a bed of pine needles.

"And that," I groaned, "is why I hate flying."

As if timed to absolute imperfection, Vicky's phone began playing the theme tune to Wonder Woman. She was getting a call. I let down the shield, released her from my hug, and she fumbled out her phone as I rolled onto my back and lay very still.

"Hello?"

I could hear mumbling and shouting from the other end of the line. The Slug. Damn, what was his name again?

"Sorry, sorry, I got caught up in, er, work."

More shouting, Vicky's face flushing the longer the tirade went on.

"I didn't know," she said, checking her watch. "Of course I'll be there to take them to school. When have I ever missed doing that?"

More shouts.

"Apart from those times? I'll be there soon, just make them breakfast and get them ready please, but I'll take the girls to school like I always do." Vicky hung up. I pulled a twig from her unraveling ponytail.

"Do not," she warned, "say a word."

"Wouldn't dream of it. Shall we steal a car?"

"Yes." Vicky's eyes didn't even sparkle with excitement. When it came to her kids, she took her responsibilities very seriously.

A feather landed on my knee where my combats were ripped.

Mom Stuff

The drive took hours that felt like many torturous lifetimes stuck in the most devilishly devised of hells. I knew that when I finally died and got stuck on a loop in my everlasting afterlife this would be my punishment. To forever repeat this journey, to speed across the country on its network of motorways, setting off every speed camera, my body hurting, my mind screaming, wishing I was back in the helicopter, anywhere apart from in a stolen car with an utterly manic, completely stressed-out, jabbering, intermittently screaming, sometimes yelling into the phone, Vicky.

Yeah, we were late picking the kids up for school, and Harry, a.k.a. the Slug, was not happy.

Neither was I.

I had my own set of problems to worry about. For one, I had to cancel the exchange with Ivan, and you shouldn't piss off gangster vampire werewolves for obvious reasons. Two, we'd just killed Nathan, and Cerberus probably wouldn't take kindly to that, especially as they knew I knew all about the warehouse now. Three, if what I thought was in the silver box in my barn belonged to who, or what, I thought it did, it was very, very bad to have not got rid of it at the earliest possible opportunity, as the true owner, and not the guy I stole it off, seemed to have somehow known I was going to take it before I had. That's the problem with such entities, they can be anywhere, any time, and this one had obviously been keeping its eyes and ears open for any mention of the book.

But, and it made everything else pale into insignificance, the worst thing of all was Vicky screeching and sobbing, shouting and generally giving me abuse for not driving faster. When we got stuck in traffic just a few minutes from her home I honestly thought my head would explode. I wished it would. Brains splattered all over the plush interior of the Mercedes Benz would have been preferable to listening to her moaning a moment longer.

"Told you not to come," I said. "Not when there's school in the morning."

Vicky turned her cold gaze on me and the pressure built. Her neck turned puce, her cheeks swelled until she looked like a rabid chipmunk, a thick vein throbbed at her temple, and I only just ducked in time as she punched out fast and hard.

"You're the one who took me to see Beast. You're the one who crashed the helicopter. This is your mess."

I shrugged. "I'm a bloody gangster, this kind of thing happens all the time. You know that."

"Do not."

"And besides," I offered brightly, "you're the one who killed Nathan. So, nah."

As my nose split and blood splashed onto the cream leather, I realized this wasn't the right time to have that discussion.

Ten minutes later, with a tissue stuck up my nose and Vicky in tears, I pulled up outside her house. The Slug was on the doorstep, tapping his foot. His obese body rippled under his crisp white shirt.

Vicky flinched in the car, looking truly worried. "You okay?" She nodded. "He'll understand." With a pout, she got out then bent to say something.

I burned rubber to the shout of, "You coming in?"

Like hell I was.

I went straight to the only place I knew I could go and not get shouted at by women.

Satan Breathes

"You know it's after you, right?" said the Turk as I approached the small counter at Satan's Breath.

"What! How the hell do you know? You sure?"

The Turk rolled up a towel and placed it with the rest behind him on a new shelving unit. Guess he was doing minor renovations, first I'd ever seen. His thick mustache twitched as he smiled and his belly wobbled underneath his stained white vest. He was way too hairy to walk around like this, but it was his place, his rules. He nodded, dark eyes dancing.

"Damn. What's so funny? And how do you know stuff like this?"

"Because I'm the Turk."

"Whatever, just give me a towel. A clean one. No stains."

The Turk handed me one that actually smelled nice, like lemons, and I snatched it off him and went off in a huff into the changing rooms. Goddamn it. If he could sense this thing after me, I was in deep do-do. Why'd I have to get greedy and take this job from Ivan?

And that was another thing. He must have known what I was getting for him. Meaning, Mikalus definitely knew, so they'd put me in this position knowing the likely outcome. I'd have to have a word. Politely, of course.

But first things first. I needed to chill, or sweat. Relax, I needed to relax. I waved away the wards guarding my locker, ignored the artifacts I kept stored there even as they turned the air blue with magical pleas of release, stashed my clothes, and wrapped the towel around my waist. It was with calm descending that I put my hat back on my head, set it to circulate icy air around my scalp, and prepared to get sweaty.

The main room was quiet. It was early and wizards aren't usually early risers apart from yours truly, so I had the place almost to myself. The large pool —recently redone after an incident with a demon that ruined the tile work—was bubbling and just right to slow-cook the flesh off your bones, the air was thick with steam, and everything felt right with the world if only for a short while.

Over the next ten minutes I slowly lowered myself into the water, watching with interest as my skin shone pink then puce, but got myself in and leaned against the side, coming to a slow boil. I sweated out the poisons of the city and my own warped mind and actions as my pores opened, until the noxious vileness of the modern world clouded above me, leaving me free and lightheaded.

I ached on just about every level, from muscle down to bone. Even my ears hurt, but that was probably from listening to Vicky. But this was Satan's Breath, palace of wonder for wizards such as I, a realm of true steam magic, and soon enough the effects of the workout, the running, the crashing, and whatever other nonsense had gone on—much of it already feeling like a disturbed dream—slowly faded as the heat eased the hurt until I drifted on a sea of scalding purity that scoured me clean and scrubbed away the madness if just for a short while.

So, I'd taken something I really ought not to have taken, nothing new there, and now the true owner was after me. I just had to go get it, give it to Ivan, and that would be that. It would be his problem then, nothing more to do with me. Looking at it like that it didn't seem so bad. I'd drive to the portal, do a quick trip home, take the book to Ivan, get paid and get on with my life.

But what life was that? Be a father? I was doing that, wasn't I? George didn't want me hanging around, she had her own life to lead and of late that had meant a lot less of me. But I could keep the house in better shape, ensure I was always there for meals. Look what happened when I took jobs. I'd missed breakfast again, hadn't even called, had I? I tried to think back but my memory was foggier than the room I was in. I had a vague recollection of calling George, but that could easily have been another day, another level of madness.

Maybe I should be a stay-at-home-dad, but that was for when your kids were young, not when they were maturing women with their own lives to lead. Take it easy, focus on the vegetable plots? Get more animals? I did all that stuff anyway, it wasn't like I worked all the time. Sometimes there were weeks or months when I did nothing but hang out with Vicky or stay home and focus on improving my magical abilities. Something I'd neglected of late, ever since Vicky became properly involved now I came to think about it.

I smiled at the thought of her nuttiness, not that I'd been smiling earlier, mind you. She was something else that one, a tiny bag of bonkers. Mad as a box of frogs and then some.

Maybe I could take up a new line of work? Something less dangerous? Haha, who was I kidding? This was who I was, the choice I'd made, and I had many years ahead of me if I didn't get myself killed for the final time. Maybe hundreds of years. What else was I gonna do but mix with the undesirables and steal magical items for high-paying clients? I wasn't about to go back to the wayward life of my younger days, where I was more a bodyguard for the major players both magical and not so magical. Those days were behind me and it hurt too much when I got hit anyway. Let the youngsters do that nonsense.

No, I was old enough, certainly ugly enough, to admit the truth about myself and my future. I was, and would always be, The Hat. And The Hat did whatever the fuck he wanted to.

I sank under the water, then came up spluttering and swearing. I'd forgotten to take my bloody hat off my head.

Time to go home and get this stupid bloody debacle over with. I'd tell Ivan that we were through, no more jobs for the vampires. I'd tell him without getting angry, of course. I may be The Hat, but I'm not stupid. Not all the time, anyway.

Dirty Again

Exfoliated to within an inch of my life, pores tight from a cold shower before I boiled, hat dried off with a touch of magic, and feeling semi-human again, I passed the Turk giving an ancient wizard grief for blow-drying his balls in the locker room—it was about time someone set the old dude straight, what is with that?—and exited Satan's Breath.

Cracked concrete and dilapidated buildings greeted me in this part of the city, familiar and comforting in their own way. A breeze ruffled my long hair and tickled my beard—I needed some serious grooming but to be honest I just couldn't be bothered. It wasn't like the women were queuing up to fondle my bits, in fact it had been so long I wasn't even a hundred percent sure I still had bits down there. Maybe the old dude knew something I didn't, and I should get a hairdryer?

Distracted, I didn't notice the chill until my teeth began to chatter and my eyelashes felt frosty. I brushed at my eyes and breathed deeply through my nose, the icy air stinging my nostrils.

"Great, what now?" I muttered, willing the magic that had gathered inside me while I rested in the pool to ready for action. I was far from on top form, needed at least a half day in my Quiet Room and to focus properly for that to happen, but I'd made do with less in the past so what was a poor, charming, heroic wizard to do?

I peered forward at the rippling concrete and the weeds that froze even as I watched, then one flattened with an audible crunch and I whipped out my wand and sigils activated as warm air gushed from the tip to counter what was, I was sure, a very poor veil.

Orange heat highlighted a ball of protection several paces away then chewed through it before fizzing out in the dull morning like the dying embers of a rain-soaked fire.

"Don't tell me," I groaned. "You're the replacement, right?"

"It's the tweed, isn't it?" said the tall man with a genuinely pleasant smile.

"That and the air of smugness that surrounds you. Can you read what I'm surrounded by? It's the air of fuckoffness I'm directing right at you. So, why don't you do just that?"

"Haha, Nathan told me you were funny." He thought for a moment, a slim finger rubbing against his clean-shaven chin. "Hmmm, actually he said you were annoying and too damn good at what you did, but he did like you."

"I have that effect on people. It's the one-liners, gets them every time."

"That's not what got Nathan though, is it? You killed him. Murdered him."

"It was an accident. And besides, you lot have been after me for long enough, interfering, being a bloody nuisance."

"I could say the same about you, Arthur 'The Hat' Salzman. Is that a Jewish name? It's not easy to find out much about you."

"Fuck off, don't play games with me. I'm sure you know everything about me, or my past anyway. So, what do you want?"

"First, let me introduce myself. I'm Carmichael, Nathan's replacement."

I studied him while he spoke, but it was just more of the usual. The higher-ups in Cerberus had an uncanny knack of all looking the same even if their features were different. Carmichael was tall, six-five, with a gangly build. But he held himself with military bearing, spoke in that clipped way that told of time in the army bossing about the grunts, and clearly kept in shape.

He oozed wealthy background, private school, always knowing the right people. One of the good old boys, the kind of guy that went to private member's clubs and hobnobbed with those in positions of power. CEOs and politicians, those running the spies, those running Cerberus, probably the country, and who knew what else.

Basically, the absolute opposite of me, and I did not like his suit either. He had a neatly folded handkerchief poking out of his breast pocket, and I wanted to strangle him with it.

Carmichael raised an eyebrow at me, and I knew we weren't going to be friends. I waited him out, but he didn't frown or act annoyed, just smiled and hummed. Buster's hat, this guy was chilled. He'd probably spent years honing his waiting game as he plotted to get rid of Nathan and move up a notch in Cerberus, which was how I imagined these guys liked to pass the time.

But he also knew magic, and although hardly astounding it was better than Nathan, and he didn't seem to have anything in the form of an aid. No amulet, no wand or staff I could see, but he could have had anything concealed beneath the suit that cost more than most families earned in months of hard, honest work.

Not in the mood, I kept my distance but walked past, neither of us saying a word. I got in my car—my stolen car—and expected him to give me grief, but even as I drove off and glanced in the rearview he was still standing there, smiling, then he nodded once and disappeared behind his veil.

"Freak," I muttered, then drove through the city, preoccupied and increasingly unnerved by the meeting.

I missed Nathan, at least I'd known where I stood with him. This guy genuinely gave me the creeps. Plus I knew I couldn't go straight to the portal, my paranoia was too high, so I spent an hour driving around, switched cars three times, changed the meeting time with Ivan yet again, then finally made it to the house and portal.

My stomach rumbled as I closed the door behind me and put the wards back up, so I called Vicky and asked her what she was up to and did she want to meet for lunch. She was sullen and uncommunicative, and said she couldn't, and it was only after I hung up that I realized she hadn't even asked when we were meeting Ivan and if she could come.

Things must have gone badly at home.

So I sat alone in my pretend living room, hungry, aching, knowing things would get a lot worse, and then I must have finally fallen asleep.

I woke with a start, and luckily didn't do that jumping thing you sometimes do, because pressed against my throat was a very sharp, very shiny knife.

"Hello, Arthur," said the intruder.

"Gah," I replied, frankly a little put out as I really needed the sleep.

Surprise

"Haha, gotcha."

The knife moved away from my throat and I focused on the owner of said knife, rather than the blade itself. "Hell, Vicky," I croaked, "you scared the life out of me."

"That's what you get for falling asleep on the job. You ready?"

"Ready? Ready for what?" I rubbed at my neck, miffed that she'd pulled a fast one on me, and tried to clear my befuddled head.

"For the exchange. Have you got the book? Where is it?"

"Um, no, not yet. I crashed out, couldn't keep my eyes open. What's the time?"

"Three. I've got until eight. The kids are at a party right after school and hubby is never home early on a Monday."

"Oh, er, right. Great," I said, not meaning it at all. "Exchange is at four, I just need to go get the book." I shouldn't have slept, but couldn't help it. The night had been wild, the workout intense, not to mention the helicopter and such like. Damn, what a busy time of it.

Vicky stared down at me, hands on hips, tight red sweater with weird little white pom-pom things on it making her look like a diminutive clown. The sleeves were rolled up, clearly too long, and the neck was strangling her. "Nice jumper."

Vicky beamed. "The girls made it for me. They learned in school. I helped a little, but they did most of it." Vicky twirled, like I actually cared, but I made all the right noises and only grunted when I got off the sofa.

"Very stylish. How are you so perky? Aren't you sore? Knackered?" My legs felt cramped and my upper body just ached in a nice way, but I was so exhausted I could have dropped back to sleep no problem. Even with the damn book making me more or less a sitting duck if the owner got a whiff of it. It was best where it was until the last minute as far as I was concerned.

"I had a nap. And I ate. I was starving. Beast was a good idea, I'm still famished."

"That's great. See, told you." My stomach rumbled angrily at the mention of food and it was then I noticed the paper-wrapped parcels on the table, grease seeping through. I sniffed and my hunch was right. "Fish and chips?" Vicky nodded with a wide-eyed grin. "Awesome. You're a lifesaver."

We sat and opened up the goodies to reveal crisp cod in batter, and tons of chips soaked in vinegar with enough salt to turn a pool into an ocean. The heat seeped through and warmed my legs and soon my stomach was feeling just as toasty.

"Hey, how'd you get in?" I asked between mouthfuls.

"Just knocked and the door opened."

I coughed and spluttered and tipped food everywhere but managed to grab hold of the paper and the beautiful battered cod as I leaped to my feet. "And you didn't think to tell me?" I scanned the room in a panic as I sent out feelers for my wards. They were down. Gone.

"Shit."

The room was plunged into darkness. Vicky screamed. I stuffed food into my mouth as fast as possible.

Time to Go

I swear, I was gonna give Ivan a piece of my mind for getting me involved in this shit. The one thing I'd learned over the years was that you don't mess with entities that get this worked up about a bloody book. And why now? Why was it picking on me? What about the dude I nicked the book from? Why hadn't he had this kind of grief? Why hadn't the book been taken from him by this most terrible of beings?

Hopefully, I'd find out, but to be honest I didn't care that much, just wanted to get out of this spot of bother alive, go get the artifact and deliver it, shout at Ivan, and then I was definitely—this had made my mind up—going to take a nice long break from any of this nonsense.

Maybe I'd get myself together, have a shave, even go to the barber's, and buy some new clothes. It's one thing having a certain look, but constantly wearing either jeans or combats and the same sweaters, shirts, and jackets every day did get tiresome after a decade or so.

Yeah, that's what I'd do, I'd have a makeover. Haha, maybe there was something that could be done about the wrinkles, some special cucumber or something that I'd put on my eyes while I relaxed in a spa so I'd emerge looking ten years younger, feeling completely rejuvenated.

"Arthur!"

Vicky's scream broke my untimely ruminations, so I snatched out for her and brushed against something soft and giving.

"Hey, you pervert," squealed Vicky.

"Sorry, grabbed the wrong bit." I moved my hand lower and felt along a bony arm for her hand. With fingers entwined, I whipped out old faithful, was about to say something smart and full of innuendo, but could think of nothing witty, so instead used my wand as a light source and dragged Vicky as fast as I could into the hall.

"I WANT IT," came a familiar voice. The sound had no source, was everywhere and nowhere, a favorite party trick for immortal, powerful beings when they come to play with frail humans.

"Don't we all," I shouted back as we ran. "I was thinking a haircut and some new clothes. Maybe that's what you need too."

"RETURN WHAT YOU STOLE. OFFER IT FREELY."

Space began to feel warped, like we were being dragged away from one plane of existence and into another. Not in a nice way, where you'd get to understand the power of the cosmos, maybe unlock the secrets of the universe, that kind of thing, but in a screwy way that I knew would send us loopy.

"What if I don't?" I asked, unable to help myself. This was odd, why not just take it? I guess it couldn't sense where it was, so it had its limits, wasn't all-seeing, but the offer it freely thing struck a chord. What could this being actually do? Oh yeah, crash helicopters. But wait, we hadn't crashed because of it, had we? No, it had merely scared us, but we didn't die.

"THEN I SHALL DESCEND."

"And that's bad, right?" I asked, hoping maybe it would mean we could settle it like men. Or like man and insanely powerful and scary thing.

"RIGHT."

Thinking now was a great time for a change of scene, I carried on dragging Vicky's slick hand and with a little yelp from my red-sweatered amigo, we plunged through the portal and emerged in the barn.

There was a whoosh of an unfamiliar kind and I shoved Vicky forward and away as I felt something like a thick rubber band around my entire body yank me back toward the portal. This was a first, and not in a good way. I fought with an inner strength mainly forged from stubbornness and tinged with annoyance, and struggled to walk forward as I was pulled back.

The gate crackled and spat out white light, which couldn't be good for it, but I refused to be sucked back in. With a final setting of my teeth and a surge of magic, I broke free and smashed into the ground.

The portal was silent, nothing to see there as I turned, so I hauled myself up and ran into the main barn only to find Vicky there with her arms raised, looking up.

Black feathers drifted, silent and beautiful, calm and quiet like the first snow of winter. Everything was still and perfect and beautiful.

And deadly.

About Time

"Do not touch them," I warned as Vicky tried to grab the delicate feathers.

"Why not?" She lowered her hands though, and turned her attention to me rather than the impossible black cloud amassing above.

"Because I have no idea what it might do to a citizen. Heck, I'm not even sure what it will do to me, and I've already touched a few. Maybe it puts you on his radar or something. Dunno." I didn't, and it was annoying. This dude had been chasing me for a while now, but in a weird game of cat-and-mouse. I was missing something, couldn't understand why he didn't just come and make me return the book. Something was off.

"And who is he? What is that thing? Can it kill us?"

"Not sure who exactly. What it is is best not said right now, and as to if he can kill us, then I'm not too sure about that either. I thought he could, but maybe not. We didn't die when he attacked the helicopter, but maybe that was because he wanted the book back."

"This is all about the book?" Vicky turned and stared right at the place I'd hidden it.

"Bloody noob," I muttered. "I knew you'd peeked. What's wrong with you? You don't look where you've hidden something, it gives the game away."

"But he's not here," whined Vicky.

"How do you know?" I asked, looking up at the dark cloud and the falling feathers.

Vicky looked up too and then I snapped out of my stupor and ran to get the silver box before anything stupid happened.

Retrieved, I ditched the box and pocketed the book after sealing it tight. Always prudent to protect your stolen goods. "Right, now we just have to get back to the city, meet Ivan, and be done with this shit."

"I am not going back through that portal. That thing is on the other side."

"Well we can't drive, it will take too long."

Vicky thought for a moment, then frowned. "I have to get home for the girls later. Harry will go mental if I'm not there when he finishes work. He wasn't happy this morning, we had a huge argument."

"Not surprised. You were supposed to take the kids to school. You should keep better time."

"Arthur, you're supposed to be on my side," protested Vicky.

"I am, but you have to get your priorities right. You wanted in to this life, but you don't have to get involved in every damn thing I do."

Vicky smiled despite her concern, and said, "You'd be lost without me."

"Oh, yeah, sure. I didn't have a clue what I was doing until you came along."

"Still don't," she mumbled.

As we bickered, the air around us fizzled and shone as sparkly loveliness filled the barn. I half expected the sound of a harp or maybe soothing chamber music, but I made do with a smile.

"About time," I said as faery dust began to fall and everything felt that much better in the world.

"Hey, Dad. Hey, Vicky," said George, looking, well, looking beautiful beyond compare. Faery dust fell from her lustrous auburn hair like summer dew catching the rays of the sun on a perfect day. Her eyes glistened like infinite pools of clear water, revealing a purity of soul and mind no human could ever hope to achieve.

As she moved, her limbs shed tiny motes of magical dust that shone impossibly bright, and everything felt right in the world if only for a moment.

Then George frowned and her whole body shuddered and static broke up the image like the freeze-frame on an old VHS movie. Lines split her body and the space around her as she flashed in and out of existence.

Then the atmosphere became truly charged with otherworldly purity and faery dust fell in earnest. George's image flickered once more then was solid. Standing beside her was the most beautiful woman you could ever hope to set eyes on.

Sasha rested her perfect, utterly lickable fingers gently on George's shoulder and said sweetly, "What did I tell you about controlling the ether as you manifest?" She smiled lovingly at my daughter, less a chastisement than direction from one with infinite patience. When it suited her. I'd also seen Sasha do despicable things that would make the most hardened of war criminals squirm. That's the fae for you.

"Sorry, I thought I had it this time."

"Look, it's great to see you're bonding so well and that you're learning so much, George, but if you've come to save us then can we get on with that? Like, now?"

The dark clouds gathered again and the feathers fell, catching faery dust as they drifted.

Sasha frowned at the interference and said, "They're such a nuisance. Did you know that once I had to actually—"

"Later, all right? Let's go," I said, staying calm and not snapping at my faery godmother at all.

Sasha turned her full attention to me and said, "Arthur, what have you been up to now?"

"Er, nothing much. Blame the vampires. Blame Vicky's brother."

"And it has nothing to do with you? You didn't take something? Is that a book in your pocket or are you pleased to see me?"

I glanced down, and mumbled, "Yeah, it's a book." It was, honest. Sasha can have that effect on you, but my daughter was right in front of me, and ugh, gross.

"Very well, let's go. Vicky, Arthur, please hold a hand each."

Sasha and George held hands and I held Sasha's left, Vicky held George's right. Magic, true, pure, incredible magic surged through us all and we were connected in a way impossible to describe.

"Now, George," said Sasha sweetly. "Remember to focus, and as this is your first time bringing anyone to Faery I suggest you be very careful. We don't want any accidents."

"Um, wait," I stammered. "Maybe this isn't such a good idea."

Then my body got ripped apart by the universe itself. Which didn't feel nice in the slightest.

Things Get Freaky

"Everyone feeling okay?" asked George nervously as we let go of each other. For me and Vicky it was because the pressure was building in our heads and we were screaming, Vicky louder than me of course. I was an old hand at this, not that I ever liked it.

"Been better," I grumbled.

"Argh," said Vicky.

"Well done!" said Sasha, beaming with pride at my daughter, who, in return, grinned like the Cheshire cat.

"Ugh, what was that about being careful and this being your first time?" I asked, trying to keep my mind off where we were and instead focused on something I understood.

"She needs to learn," said Sasha. "And that was as good a time as any."

"And I did it!" George did a little slow dance shuffle type thing, faery dust sparkling in all the colors of the rainbow as the land of Faery shimmered and shone and generally freaked me out.

"Argh," said Vicky again.

Sasha went to her, whispered in her ear, then gently stroked her head. Vicky calmed in an instant and soon she was breathing normally and looking quite chipper. Nobody rubbed my head, or any other part of me.

"Now, Arthur," said Sasha as she turned to me with her hands on her wondrous hips, pressing tight against some figure-hugging spangly material that shone gold, catching the light from George's green dress in the same, way-too-tight and my-daughter-shouldn't-be-allowed-out-like-that cut. "What exactly was that all about? It's a good job we were there to rescue you. Don't you think it's about time you stopped annoying such entities?"

"I didn't know who it rightfully belonged to when I took it. How could I?"

"Maybe you should have done your research. I thought that was what Vicky was for, to help you with these things?"

"Yeah, Vicky, why didn't you know?"

"Know? Know what? I still don't know what's going on, who that was. What's with the feathers? Is it trying to kill us?"

I waved away her moans and asked Sasha a rather important question. "Can it kill us? Will it?"

"Depends," she said with a frown.

"On what?"

"If anyone is stupid enough to give it what it needs to actually return in physical form. You aren't that stupid, are you, Arthur?"

"No, of course not!" The nerve of this woman. "Um, and just out of interest, how would one go about giving it what it needs to manifest as a physical entity? Because, even without a body, it's almost killed us in a helicopter, and then I had to fly the bloody thing. And then we really did crash it."

"You flew a helicopter?" asked George, shocked and very impressed as it's a cool thing to do. Even for a dad.

"Yeah," I said glumly.

"I thought you hated flying?"

"I do. So we crashed. Don't worry, we didn't die." All three women stared at me funny. "What? We didn't."

"You'll have to tell us all about it, I'm sure," said Sasha.

"Maybe I will, maybe I won't." For some reason I was getting defensive, probably because I was losing track of things and could have sworn I'd already told George about it. When had it been? This morning? No, that couldn't be right, could it? Hell, it was. We came back to the city, Vicky got into trouble with Harry the humongous hubby, I had a sauna, and blah, blah, blah. No wonder I was bloody tired.

"Hello, anyone in there?" George waved a hand in front of me and I snapped back to reality. If you can call Faery reality. And that reminded me, this place was freaky and getting freakier.

We weren't meant to be here. Everyone was spasming. Speeding blurs of shapes that I assumed were fae moved in all directions, the landscape sparkled and was beautiful, I'm sure, but as with all these places the fae called home, I couldn't actually see it properly. It was ephemeral, just out of reach, hidden behind a veil that left mortals out in the cold.

Was I a mortal? Sasha had given me extra lives, so I wasn't just a citizen who knew magic. I was a damn wizard and had argued with Death himself on numerous occasions. Surely I should be allowed a little peek at the places they called home?

I longed for it, wanted it, needed to belong and live here with the beautiful people. Except part of me knew that could never be, and that they may be beautiful but that didn't make them any nicer than anyone else. They could just do more, experience more, feel more, so they were extreme in personality types, hence why many had tried to kill me in one foul way or another.

I was losing the plot, getting sucked into the place and finding it hard to even remember what our world was like. This was why I hated coming here, to the real homes rather than the barren wastelands that littered the Nolands as a whole and many parts of Faery where humans could spend time without everything being all wonky.

"Okay, let's try this again," I said. "What can give it physical form? Can he really not hurt us unless he has it? Does that mean we're in the clear and all it can do is scare us?"

"It can change things, hence the helicopter," said Sasha. "But it can't let you come to any physical harm or kill you unless it is manifest. And they can't do that just because they want to. There are rules. No, someone would have to be very remiss to allow one to take on a true human form."

"Which is?" I asked, getting annoyed.

"Leaving open access to places of magic, calling them by name and summoning them. Letting them tap in to true magic that is off-limits where they come from. A few other things."

"Oh, that's all right then. I'm not about to do any of that." It was a relief, I can tell you, as things had begun to get worrying. But I knew my magic, and I wasn't about to open any Paths so it could tap into something it ought not to."

"Um, Sasha," said George, the tone in her voice putting me on instant high-alert.

"Yes, my sweet?"

"I may have not closed the Path behind us."

"Oh, I'm sure you did a fine job. As long as you tried then it will be closed, that's how these things work."

"No, I mean I may have forgotten to close the Path at all. It's Dad's fault," she accused, stabbing a finger in my direction.

"Hey, what did I do?"

"You distracted me. I was all excited to be saving you and Vicky and I, er, well, it was my first time taking anyone along a Path I've made, let alone into Faery."

"It's time to go," said Sasha hurriedly, looking about as panicked as I'd ever seen her. Which meant, she moved with total grace but faster than usual, still utterly unruffled.

"No, if he's coming then I'll deal with him. Can you close off this end so he gets stuck back home?"

"She can, so can I," said Sasha, affronted.

"Then do it, now. Send me back, you stay here."

Sasha nodded, knowing this was not something to discuss further. She wafted a hand and a portal opened, sparkling and black and then bright as the sun. I stepped through without pause, but something grabbed my jacket and I knew as my hand was gripped that it was Vicky. She never did do as she was told.

Too late to protest, the Path slammed shut behind us. We split apart into constituent elements, pinged back together and into the barn exactly where we'd been before George and Sasha arrived, and I watched as the portal, Path, whatever the hell it really was, closed without a sound.

Just as it did so, it spat out a tiny black dot, so small anyone else would have missed it. But I was looking for something, maybe the owner of a book that had entered the beginnings of Faery but had been trapped, but now it had been opened to send us back, it had returned too, and that meant only one thing.

"Run," I shouted, and legged it for my own private portal. I had to get rid of this book. Fast.

Laughter boomed, echoing off the barn's interior, sending dust streaming down from above as the wall to the back room collapsed and with it access to the portal.

We turned, facing nothing but shadow in the dark gloom, and then something stirred.

Feathers danced in the frigid air.

"I don't think you'll make it home for supper, Vicky."

"Me either."

A Ruse

"Stay here," I ordered Vicky as I untangled my hand from hers and stepped forward. She didn't argue.

"Okay, okay," I said, hands up, knowing there was no choice.

"You will return what is mine?"

"Of course, you should have just asked."

The shadows shifted as if the being was thinking. I'd said it before, and I'll say it again, angels have no sense of humor. "I did." Did I mention this was an angel? No? Well, it was. One of the most despicable, horrid, annoying beings in all of creation. Smug too, because, you know, the whole God thing.

"Oh, right, sorry. I forgot. I don't sleep well, keep forgetting things." Even as I spoke, all I could think of was if George was okay. I hoped she didn't feel too much to blame. It wasn't her fault. Okay, it was, but only this bit, the rest was on me. I took responsibility for anything that happened involving magic or my job, and I'd undoubtedly brought this down on myself. Hopefully, she wouldn't be too upset about her role in this. She'd done pretty well, especially for a newbie to the whole faery thing.

"Give," came the voice, growing in maturity as the shadow evolved, fanning out as it took on energy, feeding on the magic it had ingested and absorbed from the Path to Faery.

"Sure, it's over there, in the box. See, it's on that hay bale."

Shadow too dark to be real shifted and I caught a silhouette of a face. Vicky gasped but I didn't turn to reassure her. This was a deadly business and I didn't want to spook anyone. The silhouette morphed and changed, horns receded, facial features popped out from the square-jawed blocky outline then stretched into something slender and elven, probably handsome knowing the damn angels.

It growled in anger but moved nonetheless, heading straight for the silver box. No doubt recognizing it, believing its quest was over. The angel moved slowly, cautiously, constantly checking on me and Vicky and the barn in general. Once it got close enough, it snatched out fast with an arm that stretched the shadow, taloned fingers wrapped around the box then took on true human form, and at that point I pulled my arm from behind my back, shunted every ounce of will and magic I had into my wand, and the sigils activated in a very specific and very unusual, very seldom used sequence.

I let rip.

The shadow creature-cum-angel, and still not quite a person for the time being, ripped from the real shadows with an audible tear and zipped into the box. I slapped my wand toward the ground and the lid snapped shut.

Then I breathed.

Wasting no time, I turned and blasted the rubble, clearing a path to the portal, undamaged as not even angels can ruin something like this. "Come on," I shouted to Vicky, and she hightailed it after me.

"Was that a—"

"Yes, an angel. And now it's a very pissed off angel. So let's go."

I grabbed her, pulled her through, and shoved her into the kitchen.

"Make yourself comfortable for a while. Don't forget to be home for your family."

"Arthur, don't you dare," she warned.

"Sorry, but it's for your own good. Look after yourself. And it's been fun, Vicky. Honest it has. Sometimes. Love you."

With that, I spun on my heels and plunged straight back through the Gate of Bakaudif to try to reason with what I imagined would be a very miffed, and already escaping angel direct from heaven itself.

Barely Contained

I clambered over the carnage of the wall and ran cautiously into the barn. It was getting properly dark now and the light of the portal still flashed across my retinas, half-blinding me. I took a moment to adjust, forcing fading magic into my vision until the after-effects cleared. It didn't help much, the dull weather and the encroaching dusk made everything take on a pallid, monochrome hue.

All apart from one place. The silver box was vibrating on the bale of hay, white light spat and arced from the poor seal, the lid rattled, and the howls of one very pissed off angel deafened me. I summoned all I had left, stepped forward knowing there was no time to reconsider or think of a better plan until I knew he was going to stay put at least for a while, and I let my mind clear.

Instead of worrying about family and friends and faery godmothers, I summoned up images of carefully constructed sigils in my mind until they manifest as light in the air. Glowing silver shapes that meant nothing to anyone but me, the mental images I'd perfected over years that held special significance, contained magic and spells, danced in the air.

Magic may be a mental game, controlled by your will and determination, but you need to give that power form of some kind. These sigils held many spells each, contained direction and instruction imbued with forces that would see me ripped apart if not perfect. No need to speak the spells to get the magic to do my bidding, though it could be reassuring at times. The images themselves contained the words, my many hours of isolation while I practiced and made countless cautious mistakes until I got them right.

They wobbled and wavered and I forced the last of my energy into them until they became almost solid things. Then they shrank as the box vibrated and the angel howled its anger. With a flourish of the hand, I sent them to the lid and they slammed it shut as they settled into the silver, etching themselves deep.

Then I breathed.

All was silent, all was dark. All was not well.

A Delivery

I called Ivan and asked if we could meet at his headquarters. I didn't want Candy or any innocents involved in this, and with events less than certain with Cerberus I sure as hell didn't want any more bodies piling up. Last exchange had seen Cerberus wipe out a couple of Ivan's guys, or I assumed it was them, and I frankly wasn't in the mood for such games.

What I didn't tell Ivan was what had gone down. That was his fucking problem. He agreed to the meeting although he sounded seriously pissed off—he wasn't a man to take kindly to arrangements constantly being changed and he was meant to have had the book early this morning. Tough shit, we'd been kind of busy with exploding helicopters and Cerberus and what have you. Oh, and pissed off angels.

Plus, I knew it wouldn't be long before George and Sasha showed up and I didn't want them anywhere near this being. Hell, I didn't want to be anywhere near it, but this was my mess and I'd clear it up myself. So, get it away, keep family safe, and palm off the problem onto someone else.

Namely, Ivan and the vampires. They wanted the book, they could have the bloody box it came in too.

What did I need? I scanned the barn but could think of nothing. I had my arms, I had my legs, I had my hat, I was good to go. What I didn't have was much of a plan beyond passing this major hassle on, but I felt no guilt about that. The vampires had more resources than me, Mikalus obviously knew what he was letting himself in for by requesting the book, so, in the words of a famous philosopher who's name escapes me: Fuck 'em, and fuck 'em sideways.

Nervously, I picked up the box and sent out psychic feelers to check the wards were in place and holding up. It came as a surprise to find they were. They wouldn't last long, but they should give me enough time to get out of there and give Ivan the box, and that was about as good as I was going to get. I carefully wrapped the box in a piece of oily rag I found on the ground, put it in a small leather satchel, put the book in there too, slung it over my shoulder, and marched through the gate back into the city.

The moment I stepped out the other side, my phone rang.

"Ivan?"

"There has been an interruption to our peaceful life, Arthur, and I have to deal with it immediately. Can we do this later?"

"No, we can't. You want the book, you can have it now or not at all."

There was a long silence, he wasn't expecting that. "Very well. But please push our appointment forward half an hour, if that is okay with you?"

I hated it when he was polite like this. Never trust a polite gangster, let alone a vampire you've just been rude to, it means they are seriously annoyed. "Sure, fine. But half an hour, that's all." I hung up.

The wind taken out of my sails, I did the only sensible thing under such circumstances and put the kettle on. The kitchen in this house was nice enough, basic but comfortable to use now and then when I was passing through, and as the gate was built into the arch of one of the doors leading to the garden I often stopped for a cuppa. Just instant, I hadn't bothered making it a truly homely place, but there was milk in the small fridge and right about now it sounded perfect.

I poured a cup, wrapped my hands around it, and wandered into the living room, smiling to myself as I had a little time to relax and be calm and quiet, begin to build my magic back up by taking some immersive rest in the Quiet Place so I wasn't totally tapped out and almost a citizen.

"Vicky?" My smile turned to a frown. "Bloody hell, woman, what are you doing here?"

"Woman? Who are you calling woman? What, we've gone back to the sixties have we? Should I wear a mini skirt and let you pat me on the bum?"

"Um, sorry, didn't mean it like that."

"That's what all the chauvinists say. Watch it."

She had a point, so I changed the subject. "You're meant to be on your way home. You can't stay here, it's too dangerous."

Vicky stood defiant, like an angry gnome, chest heaving in frustration, white pom-poms jiggling comically. "Did you stop it? What happened?"

"It's in the box, for now. But it's dangerous as all hell. You should leave."

"No, we're a team, and I'm not going anywhere." Vicky glanced at her watch. "Um, not yet anyway. I've got an hour then I have to go home. But until then."

"Until then, what? This isn't safe. I'm almost out of magic, there's an angel in my satchel, and Ivan's busy for a while. I need to rest, get some magic inside of me, then go give Ivan exactly what he deserves."

"You are not going to give my brother a murderous angel," shouted Vicky, her protective nature seemingly having transferred from me to her insane brother.

"He knew what the book was, knew how dangerous it was. He didn't tell me, he didn't tell you. How's that for brotherly love?"

Vicky frowned and her shoulders sagged. "I hadn't thought about that."

"I have. He deserves this. We don't." I sipped on my coffee, watching Vicky as she seemed to shrink and fold in on herself. I hated seeing her like that, it really got to me, as I knew that above all else she craved intimacy and deep relationships and it wasn't something I found easy to give.

She so wanted everyone to open up, to share emotions and for us all to be a true family. I wanted that too, but it wasn't how I was wired. I hardly ever spoke of my past or my feelings as I'd spent too long alone, too long putting up this grim facade so I could beat down the bad guys and face the hardest criminals without flinching.

"Did I ever tell you how I came to be a wizard?" I asked.

"No!" Vicky was instantly animated, eyes wide and ears practically waggling she was so keen to hear.

"If I tell you, do you promise to go home afterward? I want you to be there for your family. You need to start thinking about how dangerous this stuff is."

Vicky considered her options. "Deal," she said.

We shook.

"Let's go into the kitchen, I need more coffee."

After the coffee was poured, we sat at the simple pine table and I became lost in thought, fiddling with my hat.

"A long, long time ago," I began.

The Hat

"Arthur, stop messing with your hat!" Vicky glared at me, the excited mood somehow having vanished.

"Hey, whoa, what's your problem? I'm about to open up here and you're all angry."

"Because you're doing what you always do. You're stalling. You're trying to think how to tell me things without actually telling me too much. I'm your friend, so whatever you tell me, we'll always be friends."

"I'm not so sure about that. I've got a, shall we say, checkered past."

"And I know that. I've seen what you can do, I'm involved in it too. I've killed people."

It was true, she had. Some on purpose, others because of her shift. You wouldn't think it to look at her, but Vicky was stone-cold at times.

I stared at my hat, my very personal hat, then put it back on my head and glared at Vicky.

"What's with the hat anyway? I know it's how you got your nickname, but well, it's just a hat isn't it? I know, magic, blah, blah, but you could make any hat magical. Right?"

"Yeah," I grumbled, "but this is my hat."

"Ah, is it the hair?"

"Huh?"

"You know, the gray?"

"I am not going gray!" I protested. "And anyway, it's distinguished."

"Whatever." Vicky stood and made another coffee and I winced but tried to hide it as she turned. I stared at the spillage on the otherwise pristine counter, then at the drawer full of tea towels. "Just clean it up, you utter freak," she sighed as she carried the coffees to the table.

So I did.

Nerves settled, I sat opposite my troublesome sidekick and sipped.

"So, what's with the hat? If you're gonna stall telling me how you became a wizard, tell me about the hat."

I sighed, but figured it was about time she knew a little more of my history. And anyway, I'd started this. I wanted to share, it would do me good to open up, but it wasn't easy. Harder than sitting in a room with an incensed angel in your satchel. "Okay, but this is strictly between us. Nobody can know. I've never told anyone. Understand?"

Vicky leaned forward, eager beaver that she was. She loved gossip and secrets, lived for this stuff. "Scouts honor." She smashed her salute into her head then rubbed at the red mark.

"Muppet."

"Beardy."

"Ruiner of kitchens," I countered.

"OCD to the max," she replied.

"So, my hat has been with me right from the beginning."

"Beginning of what?" asked Vicky, already engrossed.

"Since I first learned true magic. In fact, it wasn't always my hat. The tale of my hat actually ties in nicely with how I became a wizard. It's the same story."

"Whose was it?"

"Hell, can I tell this or not?"

"Sure, go ahead." Vicky took a sip and I did likewise, then I told my story.

"Some people believe in magic, but most don't. Most won't accept it as a reality even when confronted with it. They'll make up excuses, convince themselves they didn't see what they saw, all that stuff. I was different. I always believed, I think, even when young, but it wasn't until I was older, when I left home, and boy did I get out of there as fast as I could, that I truly began to see the world for what it is."

"What's that?"

"Dangerous. Anyway, I believed, felt this something inside that convinced me it was true. Okay, this bit is a long story in itself, so I'll skip it, but I searched for someone who could teach me. Not a charlatan, the real thing. I traveled, like a lot.

Everywhere. Bumming about, doing whatever to earn enough to follow the next lead, all kinds of crap a young man gets up to. And then I found him."

"Found who?"

"My teacher of course. My master."

"You never told me this." Vicky was leaning so far forward now she was almost sitting on the table.

"So? I'm not a bloody entertainment console. This is my life, my private life. But you asked." I folded my arms, annoyed, and leaned back.

"Sorry, please continue." Vicky smiled, I glared, patronizing sod that she was.

"I found a teacher, in Africa. The Sahara to be exact."

"Shut up! You didn't!"

"I did. He was crazy, obsessed, tall, skin and bone, burned black by the sun although he was dark-skinned anyway. What's the PC word for it now? Negro?"

"Arthur, you can't say that!"

"What? Hell, he was a black man, I don't know what else to say. I can say that, can't I? I'm a white dude, he was a black dude."

Vicky opened her mouth like a fish out of water but as the gears whirled she remained quiet.

"I found him, living in a cave in the bloody desert. It wasn't what you'd think, all sand dunes and mirages, nothing to be seen for miles, just sand. It was in a small village, but a nice, clean place, and many of the houses were built into the rock face. Not to be wacky, but because they were comfortable and cool. There was running water, proper plumbing, bathrooms, just like a normal house. He lived there alone, shunned most of the villagers, and they avoided him. Then I turned up. Kid in jeans and a stupid straw hat, full of himself, itching to learn how to wield magic."

"I can just imagine. Bet you had the same swagger too."

"What can I tell you? I am what I am. I knocked on his door and he opened it. When I began to speak he punched me in the face. It went on like that for about a week, which is why my features are, um, a little wonky."

"And you let him?"

"Yeah," I mumbled, rubbing at my cheek, the memories flooding back. "The way I saw it, it was like a movie. I get rebuffed by the wise elder, he gradually grows to like me, then once I've passed the test, he takes me under his wing and teaches me the wonders of the universe. Guess I had Karate Kid or something in mind, the usual story. But it didn't work out like that, not at all."

"What happened?"

"He kept punching me, and I got pissed off. I was black and blue, my nose was broken, I could hardly see, my eye was so swollen, and to be honest it just really, really hurt. So one day when I knocked and he answered and slammed out his fist, I, well, I stopped him."

"Grabbed his arm, or his hand?"

"No, his fist just paused, maybe a millimeter from my nose. I thought he was fucking with me, but then he began to strain, like really strain, and he shit his trousers and fell in a heap covered in sweat."

"Arthur!"

"What?"

"If you're just going to make things up at least make them believable. Come on, I'm not an idiot."

"That's debatable, my nosy little munchkin, but I'm telling the truth. He shouted and he moaned and then took himself off to clean up. I stood there in his tiny hallway, not knowing what to do, so I wandered into his living room. It was empty, nothing in there, just a rug and everything else bare. His Quiet Room, to access the Quiet Place. I found that out later, mind you. At the time I assumed he was either really poor or a nut-job, probably both."

"Hmm."

"Okay, fine, you don't believe me. End of story." I got up and drained my coffee then took my mug to the sink and rinsed it.

"Arthur, I'm sorry. Please carry on."

"Nope, you blew it, kiddo. No more secrets for you."

With my back to her, I smiled. Vicky would be a nightmare if I didn't finish this story, nag me incessantly, but she could stew for a few minutes. Served her right for doubting the honesty of The Hat.

The Tale Continues

"Arthur?" asked Vicky in her cutest, best-behaved voice.

"Hmm?" I kept my back to her, gave the sink another wipe, not that it needed it.

"Will you please finish the story? Sorry I didn't believe you, it's just you never share your past. It's only this last year you've told me anything at all about your life."

I turned, serious. "Because most of it is hard to talk about. It hurts. There's a lot of bad stuff buried there and I don't like to bring it up. Fine, I'll finish. But listen, there are some things I joke about, wind you up over, but I'd never lie to you about anything important, you know that, right?"

"I know. Love you." Vicky smiled, her delicate features morphing into that smile that always sparkled, and always brought a little light into my day. Pulled me from the cloud of depression I found a struggle to beat down some days. I was so goddamn tired as usual, wanted to sleep for a year. Scrap that, just a night. Have one bloody night where I just slept and didn't have to constantly try to stop my mind whirling, going over and over the past, worrying about the present, stressing about the future.

"Arthur!"

"What? Sorry, I was miles away."

"The story? Hurry up, I have to leave soon. I need to know the rest."

I made yet more coffee then sat back down and continued.

"So, his living room was empty. I didn't find out it was his Quiet Place for many weeks. After he got cleaned up, Zewedu, this was the wizard's name, came in to the room, ranting and raving, shouting and scowling, but smiling at the same time. For a young kid it was utterly bewildering and overwhelming, but I knew I was on the right path."

"Because of the punch you stopped?"

"Right. With his dreadlocks unwound they were down to the ground, and he was dripping from the shower, but he came right up close to me, and I'll never forget his bloodshot eyes, the whites all sickly yellow like gone-off milk, as he stared at me for the longest time. Then he grinned, said something in Arabic, and slapped me on the shoulder. My backpack fell to the ground and that was that, I'd moved in."

"Just like that?"

I nodded. "Just like that. It had only taken a week and repeated punches in the face. He took me on as his pupil, his only pupil, and he taught me. This isn't for everyone, Vicky, this magic, it's the strangest thing. It changes you, corrupts you, makes you confront the dark side of life, and death, always death, and once you can access the Quiet Place, feel the enormity of the universe, the power it contains, well, it's a lot to take. Most people who search and find a way to access magic, they lose control, can't handle it. The suicide rate is astronomical for young wizards, witches, anyone who gets even a glimpse of what's possible."

"I assumed it would be awesome, all that power."

"It is, and that's the problem. We all know we're kind of insignificant, a speck of dirt on the planet, and our whole planet means nothing to the universe at large. But there's a difference between knowing, and knowing, if that makes sense?" I wanted her to understand, to really understand, to imagine just a little about how I saw the world, how I wasn't like other people, never could be.

"I think so."

"Good. Zewedu pulled no punches, and within a week he'd shown me the Quiet Place, gave me a hint of its awesomeness. I was terrified, I mean truly terrified like I've never been since. It's vast and cold and empty and uncaring, and I was opened up to it like I was stripped of my flesh and my soul laid bare, and my soul was meaningless. Pointless. Nothing. It was bleak and beautiful and full and empty and power and nothing. I learned that life is precious and so important and that it means nothing and every single one of us will be dead one day and forgotten and what we do means nothing in the long run and yet every action, every single thing we do has enormous consequence that can affect the entire history of the human race for the rest of its pointless existence."

"Wow, that's heavy stuff. You're like a philosopher. Never knew you were so deep."

"Why'd you think I can't sleep. It's a lot to accept, it's a lot to fathom, and I don't understand any of it, never will. But he showed me, and I dived right in heedless, and then I tried to slit my wrists."

"What? You didn't? Not you."

"I was insane for maybe a month as he took me deeper and deeper into places humans can't even begin to understand, just us in that room of his, filthy and hungry and emaciated and cackling like madmen as he took me further into this terrifying, humbling, utterly wondrous world of magic. He taught me how to still my mind to access magic, how to let it flow through me, how to build it up and store it in simple pieces of wood, what I eventually understood was a wand, the favored tool of those like him. But it could just as easily have been a staff, or a rock, or anything. It's about making a connection, but mostly it's all in the mind. You have to believe in magic, you have to accept that you are nothing, that anything is possible and that the things you do mean nothing, but carry a heavy responsibility too. Mostly you have to believe, really believe."

"But I believe. Why can't I do magic then?"

"Because you don't really, truly, to your very core, believe."

Vicky frowned, struggling with what I was saying, which was understandable as I found it impossible to put into words what magic really was. "I don't get it. I know you can do magic, I know there are shifters, I know what I can do every month now. I do believe."

"But you also believe in your family, your kids, going to parents' evening, school sports day, making the girls their dinner, all that stuff."

"Of course I do."

"And that's the way the world works. That's normal. Magic isn't normal. It's... hell, it's magic. And you, and everyone else, can't accept that it's nothing special, that it's just another part of life, something that isn't beyond the everyday, but is the everyday. Everything, and I mean the whole lot from us to the planet, to the universe, to how cells divide and make living, sentient creatures, to gravity and physics and maths and thought and death and souls and demons and angels and fae and elves and portals and potatoes, it's all fucking magic. You can't accept that, you think magic is something esoteric, weird, special. It isn't. It's the most normal thing of all, the only thing."

"Wow, guess I'd never looked at it like that."

"And that's fine, as it should be, and don't ever change. I need more coffee. You?"

Vicky stared down at her untouched cup then said, "A fresh one would be good."

I got up, depressed but also finding that it was good to discuss this stuff. It was lonely never being able to talk about any of this, and even if she didn't understand, actually recounting my past, explaining a little of what made me tick, it was sharing the burden and it took some weight off. Maybe I'd sleep tonight.

Haha, like the evening would go well and I'd be done with all this crap.

Mind elsewhere, I suddenly found myself walking to the table with two fresh coffees, unable to recall making them.

I sat, feeling heavy, and then screamed as the face of Zewedu came hurtling toward me, eyes bloodshot and sickly yellow, a manic grin on his face. His crooked white teeth shone the purest white, whiter than they'd ever been in life, and I toppled backward off my chair and smacked my head on the tiles in this second home of mine that housed more magic than I'd ever dreamed of back when I was searching for answers. A lifetime away from a cave in a remote village in Africa where I'd lived for a year as a young man and learned just how cold and uncaring the universe really is.

As I lay there, with Zed's face hovering above me, I smiled at my old teacher.

Bump

"Arthur, are you all right?" Vicky dashed over, spilling coffee on the table, something I'd managed to avoid, and helped me off the floor.

"Fine, just had a blast from the past. Damn Zewedu will never let me forget what I did." I stood and nodded to Vicky and then righted my chair and sat. She did the same. I gulped my coffee, took my hat from the table and put it on, hoping she hadn't noticed how sweaty I was.

"What did you do?"

"All in good time, grasshopper. Now, where was I?"

"Being depressed and saying how normal magic is, which is kind of a contradiction."

"Yeah, that's the point," I mumbled. "Anyway, he taught me, in his own, always angry, always losing his temper, and continually trying to batter me, way. He was a terrible teacher, had zero patience, but I learned anyway. He showed me how to make a real wand, how to find the sigils that resonated with me, to make them personal and give them power, and how to uncover my own style. I learned what I was good at, what I was bad at, and came to understand that at the end of the day whoever you learned from, whatever way you went about it, the end result was the same for all practitioners."

"Which is?"

"That it's all down to the strength of your will. More. You have to go beyond belief, beyond doubts and questions, and you merely have to accept. Once you do that, once you stop thinking of it as something esoteric and strange, that it's like accepting gravity or that you can breathe, then you can become a practitioner."

"That's it?"

"Yep, that's it. It's the single hardest thing in the world to master, and it's also the easiest. So, I stayed for a year, he taught me all he could, and then, when there was nothing left to be learned, I killed him."

"You what!? You killed your teacher? Why?"

"Because he wanted me to. He didn't ask me, didn't even hint at it, but the day I was to leave, as I stood there in his empty living room and he stared at me with his rheumy eyes, I knew. He nodded once, a subtle sign, and I understood immediately. Without hesitation, with no goodbyes, as he'd have hated that, I raised my wand, tapped his forehead with it, mustered my will, and the sigils I'd carved as I sat outside his front door watching the sky darken over the desert, they activated and then he dropped down dead. It was the first, and only, time he'd ever smiled. Isn't that right, my old teacher, Zewedu?"

Vicky's head shot up as I spoke and her eyes widened with fear as she took in the sight of my teacher standing beside the table wearing nothing but a dirty pair of white cotton trousers, his dark skin covered in tribal tattoos, his unruly dreadlocks hanging to the floor, his red eyes, his lips split wide in a smile.

"Make that twice. I've seen him smile twice." I nodded at the memory ghost of my teacher. He nodded back, then turned to Vicky and licked his fat lips. Then he was gone.

Vicky blanched, stared from the empty space to me in shock and wonder.

"Like I said, that's magic for you."

"Arthur, you are, without doubt, the strangest man I have ever known."

"And you, my annoying sidekick, are the most complicated person I have ever met."

"And the hat?" asked Vicky.

"Oh, right. Well, as Zewedu hit the ground his hat flew off his head. And landed on mine. And it's been there ever since. It's a mantle, a source of power, but mostly, it's a reminder."

"Of what?"

"That you don't own shit, that all is impermanence. But, most importantly of all, and this is the main reason why I have continued to wear it all these years..."

"Yes," said Vicky, holding her breath.

"Is because it's a damn fine hat."

"It does look nice," she said, and then, sitting in the kitchen next to a Gate of Bakaudif, with an angel in a box, a lonely, tired wizard hyped on caffeine and in serious need of a wee, and a tiny woman with murder buried deep in her heart and love more plentiful than any other person I have ever known, they laughed at the madness of the world and of their own actions.

What else can you do?

Some days are like this, a bit stranger than the rest. Not much, but a little.

Meeting Gangsters

I felt odd driving through the city as it wound down just as I was ramping up yet again. Unburdening myself to Vicky had been more cathartic than I'd expected. A problem shared and all that. But it had also stirred up memories I'd kept buried for a very long time, and seeing my old master again, even if it was just his ghost or an echo of his magic, had reminded me of my youth and of all that had come since.

It brought a stifled chuckle from my coffee-stained lips that made Vicky glance at me funny when I thought about how I worried about George and what she might be up to when the fact was at her age I was off in the desert shacking up with mad red-eyed men learning the secrets of the universe. Guess she was a chip off the old block.

I dropped Vicky off and she was actually early, but she didn't argue about wanting to come see Ivan. I think she was pissed at him once she thought about what this job had entailed. It wasn't that I was glad to see her go and be alone—although I was—it was mainly that I knew she was safe now. The box was playing up, and I had to keep focusing on the wards and topping them up as the angel was constantly weakening them.

So it was with much speed I drove through the city out to the wastelands of abandoned enterprise and the old factory grounds where Ivan had decided to set up his place of business. When I pulled up outside the building, I got out and spotted the usual goons dotted about, some in plain sight, others high up peering out of windows smashed long ago, and more on platforms next to rusting conveyor belts removed from the factory floor decades ago.

There were goons and several vampire goons, and I knew there would be more vampires as the true night encroached. I was getting better at keeping the vamps in my memory, even though the buggers had if not a veil, then an air of such normality that it was hard for most people to keep them in focus. There were also several vehicles that weren't to Ivan's taste. Large Hummer type things, oversized and screaming, "Look at me, I've got a big pair of bollocks and I'm a gangster." Not Ivan's style at all. He liked discreet but expensive, nothing flash or showy about his operation or the vampires' way of doing things at all. Guess this was the business he'd hinted at on the phone.

Still, I was here now, and I wanted the book gone. Heck, I didn't even care if I got paid, not right away anyway. I greeted several goons at the bottom of the steps leading up to Ivan's lair, walked up, nodded to the goon who opened the door for me without a word, and stepped into the factory. I walked across a familiar gantry, scene of much mayhem not too long ago, glanced down at the rubble and the detritus of years of kids partying, people scavenging for scrap, and remains of old equipment, plus a hell of a lot of Ivan's people, and then I was across the gantry and at the door to the mezzanine.

Should I knock? Should I hell.

I turned the handle, set my face cold, hard, and humorless—you gotta have your gangster face when you don't know what company you'll find—and breezed in like I owned the place.

And promptly stopped dead in my tracks as a familiar feeling hit the side of my head. Cold steel. The barrel of a gun pressed against my temple. I turned to face the owner, letting the barrel scrape across my forehead, and as I stared into the eyes of the fuckwit trying to intimidate me, I said, "You better either shoot me or move that fucking thing before I break your arm then smash that gun through your fucking eye." That sounded about right.

The gun owner glanced aside and much as I wanted to look to see who his boss was, I didn't shift my gaze, just eyeballed him as I heard a humorless voice ask, "Who is this joker, Ivan?"

"This is The Hat," said Ivan, sounding pissed off.

"You hear that, lads? It's the famous Hat. He doesn't look all that."

The guy still pressing the gun against my forehead sneered and said, "Looks kinda old."

"Last warning," I said. Old! The nerve.

"Your call, Price," came the voice of this guy's boss. I could picture him shrugging, acting cool like he didn't care and this was just an inconvenience.

Price smiled at me, but I saw the waver of uncertainty, a trace of apprehension. Nevertheless, he licked his lips and his finger twitched on the trigger.

I batted his arm away in the moment he hesitated, grabbed his wrist, and twisted until bone snapped. He howled in pain and I yanked the gun out of his hand, kicked him in the kneecap, and he went down. I straddled him and, gripping the gun two-handed, I slammed it down with muscles boosted by training with Beast. The barrel punctured his eyeball, spurting goop over his face, and only stopped when it hit brain.

The body twitched once then was still. A dark stain spread over the corpse's crotch and the smell of shit contaminated the air.

The room was silent as I stood and stared hard at the others. I adjusted my hat, angling it forward and to the side, then said, "You need some ventilation in here, Ivan. Stinks of lowlife."

Everyone stared at me, the boss-guy in disbelief, his goons with concern, Ivan with a blank expression. He knew how I handled shit like this, wasn't surprised in the least. I turned my attention to the new face, and asked, "What, have I got something between my teeth?"

"You motherfucker," he whispered. "That was my main guy."

"Then I did you a favor, right? If you're gonna have employees then get ones that don't hesitate."

I smiled as the rest of the guy's goons did exactly that. They should have just shot me but that's not how people act, they look for direction. These guys were so used to taking orders from their boss they probably didn't use the bathroom without him telling them to.

The guy's eyes softened and he smiled. Then he laughed, and said, "I like you. Guess the stories about The Hat are true." He came closer and slapped me on the back.

"I'm Bones."

"And I'm tired." I ignored him and asked Ivan, "We ready to do business?"

"We are. Bones here was just leaving. And, Bones?"

"Yeah?" he asked, turning from me.

"Take the corpse with you."

There was an awkward moment, a stare-down between Bones and Ivan and opposing goons, but then Bones smiled his snakelike smile again, shrugged, and said to his guys, "You heard the man, grab Price. Time to go."

I stepped aside and watched as the body was dragged out. Bones followed his men. He stopped at the door, turned, and said, "Think about what I said."

The door slammed shut behind him.

"What was that about?" I asked.

"A problem. But not one you need concern yourself with. Now, shall we finish our business?"

"You betcha."

Let's Do This

"Do you have it?" asked Ivan, sitting sideways in his Eames chair behind the old desk. His long legs were crossed and I couldn't help notice that he wore Bugs Bunny socks. His suit was immaculate, black and sharp as his cheeks, and he'd got a haircut, slick and shiny.

It could make a guy feel scruffy if he cared about such things.

"Of course I do. Why do you think I'm here?"

"Shall we?" he asked, nodding to an aide-cum-goon who hadn't moved so much as a muscle so far. The man brought over a digital device I never concerned myself with as Vicky did all the tech stuff and I put up a hand and said, "One moment." Ivan nodded at the aide and he retreated, leaving the electronics behind.

"Is there a problem?"

"The problem is that you never told me who this belonged to originally. Or, if not originally..." I faltered as it hit me that maybe angels didn't write books and didn't go dropping them down from heaven into the hands of collectors, "then someone who felt they had a better case for ownership than anyone else."

"I assumed you would do your own research. Am I to believe you don't have it? Or don't wish to make the trade?" Ivan and I had history, much of it bad, but I now considered him if not a friend then at least an ally, certainly not an enemy. Plus, he was Vicky's brother, almost family.

"We did what research we could but there was no mention of this nonsense. About who says they own it. He's been very insistent. Deathly insistent. She's your sister, yet you put her in danger."

"She has you to care for her, protect her. I know Vicky well enough to know she wouldn't bow out no matter what information I gave you. I felt it best for her to remain somewhat in the dark. And it worked."

"Worked! Are you out of your freaking mind? We almost died in a helicopter. Twice. This, ah, entity has been after us, after me, since before I even started this job, which isn't right. He's chased us across the country, he's done untold damage, and apart from all that, I make it a policy never to piss off anyone who can screw with my afterlife. Um, apart from Death, but that's different. He likes me."

"Arthur, my dear Arthur, what can I tell you? I had my orders from the First. He wanted the book, you are trustworthy, so I gave you the job. The rest was up to you. You could have refused, could have said no, but you went ahead. And besides, this is what you do. You steal dangerous things and you pass them on."

"Maybe. But I don't like it." Damn, I hated it when he made sense, took the wind right out of my sails.

"So?"

"So, you made me steal a book that belongs to an..." I stopped myself and glanced at the goons standing around the room pretending not to listen. "Um, can we have a moment?"

"Of course." Ivan nodded at his guys and they filed out politely then shut the door.

"It's an angel, Ivan. Do you understand what I'm telling you? An angel. It's his, he wants it, and he's not messing around."

"Haha, come on, I know what the book is supposed to be about, but it's not, you know, really the property of an angel. They don't exist. Do they?"

"Are you mad, dude? Of course they exist. How do you think heaven gets all its business done? This book, whatever is in it, and no, I absolutely do not want to know, not even a hint, isn't for us, any of us. Magic books are one thing, spells and the like, summoning the dead and talking to spirits, but this book is something else entirely. Ivan, you know about so much, why be surprised that there are angels?"

"Because that would mean there was a heaven, which would mean there was a God, and I refuse to believe there is a God."

"Man, you haven't got a clue, have you?" He really hadn't.

"Then enlighten me."

"No fucking chance. I'm not your social worker. You played me and we're through. This is bad business.

You don't do it like this, not if you want to keep your people on your side. I'm not saying we've fallen out, but I can't trust you guys to give me jobs that are acceptable. This was the last one."

"I'm sorry to hear that. Mikalus will be too. But honestly, Arthur, please don't take this as a personal affront from me. I just passed it on to you. I was given my instructions. I owe Mikalus my life, you owe me your daughter's."

"And Mikalus owes me his life." Okay, it was an accident, a terrible one, mainly because I did a job without knowing the full story, which sounds familiar, right? But this was different. I think.

"Be that as it may, and we both know the circumstances, he wanted you for this, so I gave you the work. Let's not argue, let's complete the transaction. I'm afraid Bones is being rather troublesome, so let's finish this so I can, er, finalize the details with him."

I knew exactly what that meant. Their meeting had gone bad and Ivan was going to eradicate him and his whole crew.

Definitely time for me to leave.

"Okay, fine. But think of your sister, man. You shouldn't let her get caught up in stuff like this."

"As I said, Vicky is willful. I wouldn't dream of interfering or telling her what to do."

"Ha, neither would I."

Knowing this would go nowhere, I took out the book and the case and laid them on the table. Should I tell him? No, he hadn't told me. Let the vampires have a nice surprise. Serve them right.

"There you go. Two for one. The book and its box. Pretty, eh?"

"Very nice." Ivan tapped away then looked up and met my gaze. "Payment complete. Would you like to check?"

"Nope, I'll take your word for it. Don't open the box, it's protected." I was going to leave it at that, but I guess I'm a real softy at heart. "It's got the angel inside, and he ain't happy. Let Mikalus deal with it, better it's safe in there than chasing me, or him, or you around."

"As you wish. I have no desire to look inside in any case. This is not for me."

"Me either. And the whole angel thing?"

"Yes?" asked Ivan, interest piqued.

"They aren't what you think they are. Don't piss them off. Or if you do, then get ready to run."

Ivan raised an eyebrow then reached across the table to retrieve the box.

As he did so, there was a series of muffled thuds from the other side of the door then it slammed open.

Bones stood there, grinning madly, covered in blood. His goons filed in around him, revealing bodies on the gantry.

"Changed me mind. I think I'll take what I want if you won't give it to me."

"So typical," I moaned.

A Mistake

I leaned back in my chair and sighed. I wasn't even particularly annoyed, not really. I'd been paid, this wasn't my problem any more. Although, I did have a reputation to maintain, and if not a friendship, then an understanding, and the last thing I wanted to do was purposely put myself on the wrong side of Ivan and the vamps.

But, and I felt daft even thinking it, the main reason I knew I wouldn't be able to stay out of this was because of loyalty. It felt ridiculous to feel such ties to Ivan, I believed I'd evened the score in regards to owing him one, or as close as I'd ever get, but he was the boss now, and I knew for sure he did a better job than anyone else I could think of. Certainly the sneering, smug looking Bones here.

So, I turned my chair sideways, tilted my hat back so he could look into my eyes, and waited. I could see Ivan with my peripheral vision, and he still had his legs crossed. This strange man was utterly at ease with what was happening. He probably expected Bones to play up after dismissing him the way he had. Or maybe he was as confident in his own abilities as I was in mine. Either way, it would undoubtedly kick off at some point, and we were both ready in our own way.

"You cut me out, Ivan, and that ain't nice." Bones stepped forward into the room and his guys spread out, trying to look menacing and intimidating, even doing a pretty good job of it if they hadn't been facing who they were. This was all way too familiar for us, seen it a thousand times before, and you can look as hard as you like, but when your face is smashed you'll still go crying off into a corner somewhere.

"I explained the situation. It's not up for negotiation. Your guys don't play by the rules, so no more territory to the east. I want the area cleaned up, not every junkie beaten to within an inch of their lives if your guys think they got looked at funny."

"Just keeping the scum in line."

Ivan stirred, uncrossed his leg, smoothed down his trousers, and leaned forward to stare intently at Bones. "The scum, as you call them, are your customers. They should be treated with respect and given what they paid for. You cut the product, you abuse the clientele, and you wonder why business is bad? You can't handle the work, you are down on your numbers, even with such an aggressive approach, so, and let me say this real slow in case you still don't understand. You are out. Finished. And after this little drama, none of you, and I mean none of you," Ivan paused to stare down each man in the room, "are leaving here alive."

"Haha, you're funny. What, two old dudes are going to wipe out me and my crew? Don't think so, old man."

"For a dead man you talk a lot," I said, giving Bones a smile.

Bones stared at me with cold, hard eyes, cruel eyes, and rubbed a hand over his shaved head. He didn't know what to make of me, or what I was capable of. I could almost see the cogs turning as he thought about how best to deal with me. He came to the wrong decision. I knew he would, I'd met his kind so many times before, and not once did it end well for them. But end it did.

He walked forward, cocky as fuck, and tried to bitch-slap me. I caught his hand before it hit, grabbed tight at his forearm, and his face reddened as he strained to move.

I let him go, keeping eye contact as he stumbled back, his hard man image broken. It pissed him off.

He pulled a gun.

Ivan sighed then said, "Bones, what the hell do you think you're playing at? You know you won't get away with this. You're a dealer, not boss material. You think all the men out there will work for you? They know what you are, same as I do."

Bones waved the gun at Ivan casually, but his men had their weapons trained on us. "They'll work for whoever pays them."

"You really haven't got a clue, have you?"

"He hasn't, has he?" I asked Ivan, knowing half of them were vampires, and Bones and his crew would be mangled bits of goo if they tried to take on the vamps.

"A growing problem with the youth," said Ivan conversationally, like we were alone and having a chat. "They don't respect age and experience, think they can do as they please. Some learn, others don't."

I nodded my head. "Some are too stupid, won't put in the proper work, always looking for shortcuts."

"Hey, hey! When you two are quite finished. What's in the box, eh? Looks nice. Worth a bit, I'd say. But antiques ain't my thing." Bones reached out to grab the box but I put my hand out and said, "I wouldn't if I were you. This is way out of your league, sonny, way out."

Bones frowned and then he slammed the gun at my head. I activated the energy stored in my hat and as the gun hit the top, Bones' arm bounced back. He yelped like a baby.

"What the fuck?" He rubbed at his arm—it would have felt like smashing into solid steel—and as he and his men were distracted I pulled out my wand and blasted a relatively subtle volley of compact shots of tight energy at several of them. They hit the floor, dead.

Bones whirled in confusion and stared in shock at the bodies, then back at me, the wand already secreted in my pocket. His surviving men lost their cool and rather than just shoot, one charged, spoiling a clean shot for the others. He roared as he sprang at me, always a stupid move as why announce what you're going to do?

Arms up, he went in for an unfriendly strangle. Not nice at all.

I sidestepped, so the bulky goon slammed into the table. As I backpedaled to avoid getting shot, the fool sent papers, electronics, a lamp, and the silver box, flying.

Bones bent and retrieved the silver box, lifting it and smiling.

"Let's have a little look-see, shall we?"

There was no time, and before anyone could say a word, Bones smirked, eyes widening as he felt the power of my magic and what it contained. Even that wasn't a deterrent, and the utter fool eased open the lid even as his hands burned and he screamed.

I ran around the ruined desk, grabbed Ivan, and simply said, "Duck."

Yeah, that's right, we hid under the desk like scared kids, and we had every reason to be scared. Especially when the screams started.

Peekaboo

Ivan and I glanced at each other as the room turned hazy, before it went dark, really dark. Then I was on my own. I knew Ivan was beside me but couldn't see him, couldn't hear his breathing, or my own for that matter, as I figured pretending not to be here was the safest course of action.

Men screamed, the air itself seemed to howl, yet the angel said nothing, made no sound, just did whatever it was doing. Stuff I knew wasn't anything I wanted to be involved in.

The room rocked to the thunder of a gun being fired, then again, and again as men let loose in any direction. The sound was deafening in an enclosed space, but it gave me a chance to peek above the table and take a gander at what was going down.

There was a blur of black, too fast to make it out, and a guy firing wildly, eyes terror-stricken. In a flash, he was consumed by the shadows. He screamed, then fell, and the shape shifted to the next man, and the next, everything stuttering as though reality itself wasn't up to the task of containing this creature.

Bones fired over and over with ruined hands, the muzzle flash highlighting his face. He was sweating badly, his left eye seemed to have developed a tic as he kept scanning the room looking for the assailant.

And he still held the damn box. Although, I think maybe that was because one hand was fused to it.

"Let's go," I whispered to Ivan.

When he didn't answer, I turned, only to find I had been talking to empty space. "You bastard," I said, just very quietly.

Bones' last remaining goon was shouting and screaming in a panic of confusion, and then the angel descended on him, his body disappearing behind a cloud of night that held impossible terrors. All I knew was it was big, and scary, and capable of doing bad things, so I took the opportunity to lunge from my hiding place. So much for it being unable to physically hurt you; it seemed to have overcome that obstacle and then some. Was it because of the magic from Faery? Or was something else at play here? The intent of Bones and his crew allowing it to hurt them? Better to ponder that later.

As the goon went down, Bones fired at the black shape, but it did nothing, as I knew it would. Distracted, I snatched the box from him, along with some of his skin, grabbed the book from the floor, put it in the box, and was out the door faster than Vicky getting a call from the headmaster that her kids had been in trouble at school.

The gantry was a sea of dead men, so I grabbed the railings either side, swung over the bodies, then ran until I slammed open the door to outside. Frigid air hit, cooling the sweat on my face, and I launched over the railing and landed in a crouch on the cracked concrete, cursing the angel, cursing Ivan, even cursing myself for bothering to return the book.

What now? Where the hell was Ivan? Where were his men?

As if in answer, Ivan came striding forward with a veritable army behind him, all the men that were tasked with protecting the area. There were a lot of vampires here now, their shift must have started, plus several grizzled, military looking, battle familiar heavy-set guys. All had serious weaponry.

"Yours, I believe," I said, holding out the box to Ivan.

He reached out a hand, not even having the grace to look sheepish for leaving me in there, but before he could take it the door blew out. The solid steel flew through the air, landed with a thud on the concrete, and Ivan was grabbed by his guys and huddled into the center of a tight ring of protection.

I was left standing there, alone, as the men spread out to cover the door while the others frog-marched Ivan toward a black sedan with the engine running. Charming.

"You should have left it," shouted Ivan. "I figured you'd be right beside me as I escaped."

"And I assumed you'd want it, and I'd have to go get it back if I left it behind."

"You know me too well, Arthur. Look after it for me. I'll be in touch." And with that he stepped inside, the door was slammed shut, and the car sped off, kicking up stones and dust as it went.

I decided there and then that my business with Ivan was well and truly done. No more jobs, no more friendship, we were over. These boss types are all the same. They see themselves as more important than the rest of us. Just because they have responsibilities, they think they are more valuable, that they can leave us grunts to do the dirty work while they get taken somewhere nice and secure and put their feet up. Yeah, maybe that's what I got paid to do, but seeing it like this, in action, brought home the fact I was in the wrong damn job.

Not wanting to be burdened with unnecessary items, I threw the case away and pocketed the book. Then the sky darkened, the floodlights began to go out one by one as they were smashed by a ragged shadow of death that flew above our heads in a frenzy of silent activity. The goons let rip with everything they had.

It wouldn't make any difference. This was a goddamn angel, and you can't just shoot them, so, while everyone else played their games, I did the sensible thing and ran for my car.

It started right up, so I drove off and didn't even put my seatbelt on, just because that's the kind of wildcat wizard I was in those days.

Safety first, kids, safety first. Do what I say, not what I do.

Emergency

My phone rang and I panicked, fishing it right out. Was something wrong with George? Surely Sasha would be keeping her safe and well away from this? I trusted Sasha, kind of, and yet my instinct was to grab my phone and begin stressing even before looking to see who was calling or if it was a good idea to take a call when I was trying to get away from a pissed off angel that wanted what I had.

"What? Are you okay? Is Sasha looking after you?"

There was silence on the other end and I swerved to avoid a cat, nearly crashing. As tires squealed and I gained control before the rear kicked out, a high-pitched voice answered. "What? Arthur, it's me. Vicky. Come quick, it's the girls. The girls!" she screeched.

There was the sound of crashing and then the line went dead.

Shit, shit, shit. What was happening? Vicky's kids? This was bad timing in the extreme, but this was my life, how things went, so I put my foot down, dropped into third, and drove as fast as the crappy car would go.

She wasn't answering her phone, and that was bad, and as I sped through the streets of the city I imagined all kinds of terrible things. Not supernatural things, just the cruel, vicious things that humans do to each other on a daily basis that make anything that happens in my own world pale into insignificance. People did inhuman things to children. They stole them, they interfered with them.

Junkies off their heads on volatile chemical compounds acted with sickening brutality without even knowing it, and the straight ones, the run-of-the-mill criminals, they were even worse. Some people simply did not care about citizens, but I did, at least about a few.

I kept glancing in the rearview but there was no sign of the angel, so either he'd lost me, or had been dragged back to where he came from. How long could it stay down here? I had no idea. I had no idea about much to do with angels, but maybe the quick wards I'd thrown up around the book were enough to give me time, keep me hidden at least for a while.

My heart was in my chest as I screeched to a halt outside Vicky's ten minutes later. I launched out of the car, ran across the street to her immaculate suburban nightmare, and stopped dead in my tracks at the chaos that confronted me. It didn't compute straight away. The driveway and perfect lawn were always a scene of domestic bliss, everything ordered and as boring as Vicky regaling me with tales of her children's day at school, but it wasn't like that now. Madness had come to the burbs in the shape of a fat man and a mini-mom.

Vicky was outside, screeching at the Slug, the doors to his boring car that he drove to his boring job were open and one of the girls was climbing out, tears streaking her face, calling for her mummy, even as the Slug, Harry, was manhandling the other sweet, innocent child toward the car. He was holding her arm tight, too tight, and she was reaching out to Vicky, saying she didn't want to go. The poor thing was crying loudly, saying he was hurting her.

"He's trying to take the girls away, Arthur. My girls." Vicky was a mess. Mascara had run down her cheeks, her slender, red dress was ripped—she'd obviously dressed up for their evening meal, trying to make amends for being absent lately—her hair was wild, and her entire body was shaking with a deep-seated fear I'd never witnessed before.

Harry was worse. His tie was over his shoulder, his thinning mousy hair was all over the place, and worst of all, the buttons on his white office shirt had pinged off under mighty pressure. His massive, pale, wobbly belly lumpy with cellulite jiggled disgustingly as he dragged the child toward the car.

He was harming her, there were marks all up her arms, and she was now limp with exhaustion and terror.

"Get back in," he screeched at a flinching child as she clambered out, unsure what to do, where to go, who to obey.

"Come here, honey," said Vicky, trying to soothe her child but her voice breaking with stress.

"Get back in, now!" Harry dragged the screaming, shaking girl toward her sister. It was clear the kids were terrified and Harry had completely lost the plot.

So I stormed over, raging, and smacked him as hard as I could right in the temple. So hard, a knuckle cracked, but I readied to do it again, my anger rising.

Harry's grip loosened and one child ran to Vicky, quickly followed by her sister. I punched Harry again once the girls were a safe distance away, amazed he hadn't gone down, giving it my all. His eyes rolled back in his head, he teetered, then he toppled sideways, smacked his head on the corner of the open rear car door, and crashed to the freshly tarmaced drive, whacking his head again. He was out, and would be for a while, if I ever let him wake up.

So help me God, I almost crushed his head with a stomp from my size nines. I was so close to doing it, to cracking his skull and letting his brains ooze out and stain his perfect bloody drive, but the kids were watching and they were freaked out enough.

Instead, I breathed deep, ignored Harry, walked over to them all, crouched down, and said, "How about we go inside? I think your dad has had a funny turn, you know, like when people eat too much sugar. Yeah, that's what it was," I said, warming to the idea. "Daddy ate too many donuts, and he can't handle his booze very well, so he's had a seizure, gone funny in the head. So never drink alcohol, let this be a warning. Or eat too many donuts." I twirled my finger at my temple, nodded to Vicky as the girls looked from me to her to their father on the drive, then stood and ushered them inside.

Vicky took the girls into the immaculate, generic living room and quietened them while I watched from the doorway. They seemed to accept whatever she told them and within minutes they were watching some show on a subscription channel apparently most people had nowadays.

"I'm just going to talk to Uncle Arthur for a minute and help him with Daddy, then I'll be back," said Vicky.

"Will Daddy be okay?" asked Tweedledum.

The innocent, trusting nature of children never ceases to amaze me, and it broke my heart to witness such concern for a man that deserved no love from such beautiful children.

"Daddy's just going to go calm down somewhere," said Vicky through gritted teeth.

"Okay, Mummy," the girls chorused, taking it all in their stride now the moment had passed.

Vicky shoved me ahead of her down the hall to the front door. She glanced outside at the body of her husband and whispered, "I want that man dead for what he just did." She meant it, and I didn't blame her.

"What the hell happened? That's not like him, is it?" I was sure he'd never laid a hand on her or the kids before, because if he had, and I knew about it, then he would have already been a dead man.

"He lost the plot, he went crazy. I got all dressed up, made a nice dinner, but he was stressed from work, more stressed than usual, and when I gave him his dinner, just us, I'd already fed the girls, he starting shouting that I thought he was fat."

"Huh?"

"Because I made him chicken and broccoli and rice. He said I was trying to run his life, make him eat rabbit food, and then he threw the salad at the wall and then... then he said I was a bad mother. Because I was late for the girls, for school. Once, Arthur, I've been properly late once for my girls in their entire lives. The few other times were just a couple of minutes. He's never here, he's always late, and I said so, and he lost it, said he was taking the girls away. He threw the bottle of wine at me, stormed into the living room, and starting dragging them outside to the car. It was red wine. It's everywhere," Vicky added, shock starting to set in.

"This is nuts, it doesn't make any sense. He's never acted like this before has he?" Vicky was silent as she stared at Harry out on the drive, and then back at me. My stomach flipped and my anger rose, but I kept myself in check, didn't let myself go wild. Not now, not with the kids there.

I put one hand on Vicky's shoulder, then the other, and I turned her so we were looking each other straight in the eye. "Vicky, I want you to tell me the truth. Has he ever hurt you or the girls? Has he ever acted violently toward you before?"

"He's... he's got a temper sometimes. He gets tired from work, he eats badly, he's very conscious of his weight, and sometimes he gets cross." Vicky rubbed at a spot just beneath the neckline of her dress and I gently moved her hand away and lowered the delicate material.

A bruise, and I'd seen enough to know how it was made. By a fist.

"Nobody ever sees," she said, and silent tears of shame fell. Hers and mine.

My heart broke for her, for all of them. You never know what goes on behind closed doors, and I knew how the world worked. How people made excuses for their loved ones, how they fought and shouted but it was all part of forging a life together. But you did not, ever, hit women, or scare your children like this. How had Vicky let this happen? How had she never told me? Because she knew I'd rip him to shreds, that was why. And, for all her toughness, Vicky loved the idea of family, loved her girls, wanted to be the perfect wife and mother, and trouble at home didn't fit with that image.

Sure, they fought and she moaned and griped about him, threatened to leave him on many occasions, but it was all just noise, or so I'd assumed. Was this why she never went through with it? Because she was scared?

"I'm sorry," I said, trying to hold back the tears, the shame, the guilt.

"Arthur, it's not your fault. It's mine."

I grabbed Vicky protectively, her body so frail and small, and I said, "No, it's not your fault. Don't ever say that. It's his and his alone. This is on him. Only him. Go pack, you're coming home with me. All of you. The girls can have a few days off school until we figure this out. Okay?"

Vicky bowed her head. I hated seeing her like that. Beaten. "Okay."

Vicky went to tell the girls, and I stood there, on the threshold to suburbia, and I cried for my friend and for the fact she'd ever thought, even for a moment, that this was her fault or something she deserved.

Fucking men.

A Holiday

"Why is Daddy still lying on the ground?" asked Tweedledee as we walked past him to my car. The girls had a small bag each, with bright characters smiling as if everything was perfect with the world, and I had a large suitcase, not the first one either.

Vicky was holding on to both girls' hands like she never wanted to let them go again.

"Because Uncle Arthur hit him because he was scaring you. It's okay, he'll be fine. He's just sleeping now, right, Arthur?" Vicky turned to me with hope as I dumped the suitcase in the car.

I turned and stared at Vicky, then the girls. "Right. He had a funny turn like I told you, and so I put him to sleep for a while with a special Uncle Arthur punch. He's fine, just resting. So, that means you get to have a holiday while Daddy recovers and thinks about what he did. You're coming to stay with me and George, how cool is that?"

The girls jumped up and down, screeching, "Yippee," even though we'd already been through all this and Vicky had repeatedly told them. Kids!

"Can we feed the chickens?"

"Sure."

"And we really don't have to go to school tomorrow?"

"Nope."

"And we can eat ice-cream all day and watch TV?"

"You cheeky sod. No, you cannot do that," I said with a smile, panicking as I wondered how I could keep them from trashing my kitchen within the first few minutes of us arriving home. We laughed as I ushered the girls into the car and got them to buckle up. I turned to check on Vicky and watched as she crossed back to the house.

She bent over Harry, then crouched down, squatting as if to contemplate her life and how it had somehow all gone wrong. I can't say I saw it coming, but something told me that things were about to get terribly out of control. I just couldn't figure out how that could be. He was out cold, the girls were safe, and Vicky was distraught but keeping it together for the sake of the kids.

I watched as she pulled something from her jacket. My guts tightened but still I couldn't quite connect what I was seeing with what I dreaded would happen. Vicky glanced around, checking on neighbors I guess, but this was suburbia and nobody had even come out. I envied them like I never had before.

Vicky adjusted her body, then her arm moved forward. I couldn't see what she did, but when Harry's body shuddered once then was still I knew exactly what she'd done. I'd seen enough death tremors in my time to be in no doubt that Vicky had just murdered her husband in cold blood in their driveway.

I turned away.

"All buckled up?" I asked the girls, checking their seat belts.

"All done."

"Roger that."

"Great, I'll be back in a minute."

Seriously?

"What are you doing? Have you gone utterly insane?" I hissed, crouching down beside Vicky. She hadn't moved, was just squatting there over her husband. Her dead, bleeding husband. His trousers were stained wet, and he stank. Death ain't pretty, even if you're pretty in life, and he wasn't.

Vicky turned to me, but her eyes were dead, vacant like she was in deep shock now. She probably was.

"Vicky?"

"He hurt my children," was all she said, then she looked from me back to Harry, all emotion drained from her.

"I know, honey, I know." I took the knife out of her hands; she didn't resist. I pocketed it as I stared at the spreading red stain on Harry's creased shirt. The cotton was stuck to his huge belly and chest like a sheet over a crumpled, dirty bed.

I felt for a pulse and then patted down his pockets, removed his car keys and found a pack of cigarettes and a disposable lighter. Damn, I didn't know he smoked. This was a mess, a clusterfuck if ever there was one. We were in the toxic center of suburbia. My paranoia kicked in. Suddenly I felt there was no way in hell that this had gone unnoticed. People would be watching; who knew what they'd seen? Maybe they hadn't seen me smack him down, maybe they had, but I was pretty sure nobody had seen Vicky actually kill him. But they could have, and I didn't know. I hated not knowing, especially when it could mean getting locked up for life. If the police arrived, I'd have to say I did it. And that would seriously suck, especially for me.

What to do?

"Wait here," I said, then walked casually into the house like everything was fine.

I emerged with a bottle of whiskey hidden in Harry's jacket then spoke loudly, feeling stupid but knowing this was best just in case the neighbors were watching. Were they, or was I right in thinking all this had happened without anyone seeing a thing?

"Fine, have another one, and here's your jacket, but you have to have it inside." I waved the bottle around, pretending like he'd gone off the rails because he was drunk. Booze can explain all manner of odd behavior, and the one thing I knew about these prim and proper suburban people was that most of them were pissed most nights to make it through to the next day without losing their marbles entirely.

I manhandled Harry into a sitting position then slipped his jacket over him, no easy thing, resorting to a touch of magic to lighten the load. Then I said to Vicky,

"We have to get him inside, just pretend like he's drunk. Can you hear me, Vicky? We have to do this now or the cops will be here. Do you want to go to prison, lose your kids?" I would never let that happen, but she didn't know that.

Vicky's head snapped around and she blinked herself back to reality. "Oh my God. What have I done? They'll lock me up and I'll never see my girls again."

"Ssh, quiet. Harry's just drunk and being stupid. Hold the bottle in his hand and act like he's drunk and help me get him inside the house. Stay calm. But hurry, the girls are in the car."

Vicky nodded. We grabbed him under the arms as I sent not inconsiderable magic down into the ground, acting as a cushion of air that buoyed Harry's gross, three hundred pound plus frame like it weighed nothing. It worked quite well, as it was hard as hell to control this cushion as we moved him with his arms slung over our shoulders, and he genuinely did look drunk. Vicky held the bottle in his hands and I even managed to control his arm enough to make it look like he was swigging from it. Somehow we got him inside.

We dropped him on the sofa and then I guided Vicky out the door and closed it behind us, all the while trying to think how to handle this and stop Vicky panicking about ending up behind bars and her girls in foster care. I couldn't tell her I'd take the blame, she wouldn't agree and would blurt something stupid if the police arrived.

I walked Vicky like a zombie to the car and made sure she was buckled in. A spark of intelligence returning to my addled mind, I stepped away and made a call.

"Cleaner," came the familiar voice.

"It's The Hat. There's a body. It needs moving, and the car too. Make it an accident. Neighbors might have seen. Can you handle it? It's Vicky's husband."

There was a moment's silence then she snapped, "I'm the Cleaner."

"Great. Payment in the morning, I'm a little busy now."

She hung up. One thing the Cleaner wasn't was a conversationalist. Vicky got on with her, even had a few chats, but Vicky could make a stone talk, so I didn't feel too bad about it.

I tried to think if there was anything else I needed to do, but was confident the Cleaner would cover this. Sure, it was gonna be a hell of a mess, but nobody had called the police so either our dodgy drunken ruse had worked or nobody had heard or seen a thing and I was being overly cautious.

Either way, the Cleaner would arrive and do what needed to be done. She'd pay a visit to every house where somebody may have been able to see, and she'd wipe the memory from them, if they had any.

I'd used her services any number of times, and it went beyond cleaning crime scenes and replacing broken furniture. She worked for magic users and was one herself, an enigma. Nobody knew a thing about her, but she was a professional, and we needed that.

There was going to be a terrible aftermath for Vicky to deal with either way, a missing persons report to file, the tears and recriminations once Harry was found, but it beat going to prison. Plus, she had me, and George, and Sasha, but most importantly she had her girls, and that was all that mattered now.

I got in the car and drove away. Nobody said a word.

Sleepy Kids

The girls were exhausted, we all were, but Vicky and I were also wired. I told her about the Cleaner and she relaxed a little, her immediate panic over with, but then the realization of what she'd done hit and with it the knowledge that her life, and her children's, would never, could never, be the same again. She had no husband, they had no father, and that changed everything. It shook her world to its very foundations.

She had, shall we say, a moment.

The girls were fast asleep within minutes, and Vicky wept quietly, but hard, beside me. All her life she'd striven to be the perfect wife, the perfect mother, dressing a certain way to fit in with the other women, keeping a tidy house, striving to conform and do what all the other middle class families did.

But it was a pretense. Vicky craved excitement and danger and had been confined to her basement to live out her fantasies, hacking into networks and trawling the dark web for kicks, and then she met me. And now she'd killed her husband. I didn't ask about what had happened in the past, she'd tell me when she was ready, but part of me still couldn't believe it, that Harry had ever been a violent man.

From what I'd known of him, and it wasn't much, he was an insecure, cowardly man. But then, all abusers were. They preyed on those weaker than themselves, took out their frustrations on their family, and he'd obviously been no exception.

Now the fucker was dead. Good riddance.

We made it to my city house without incident, which I thought was some kind of miracle. There was still the matter of the angel, the book, plus Cerberus lurking in the background somewhere, so the night was far from over. But there were priorities, and the most important thing was the well-being of Vicky's children.

We carried them inside and put them on the sofa. They woke for a moment but Vicky explained where we were and within a few minutes they settled back down. The poor things were utterly fried from the madness and confusion over how adults behaved, aren't we all, and soon were snuggled under blankets, snoring as they dreamed the dreams of the truly innocent.

I locked the kitchen door and pocketed the key, as the last thing I wanted was them wandering about and frying their brains by trying to go through the portal, then I took Vicky into the rear garden and lit up a dead man's cigarette.

It tasted divine.

I dragged like my life depended on it, pulling nicotine deep down into my lungs, and I held it there until my lungs burned. Then I exhaled, like I could blow away all my troubles, Vicky's too, and somehow make things right for us all. But I couldn't, so I smoked and said nothing, because I honestly didn't know what to say. Light spilled out from the kitchen window, sending long shadows down the lawn. I watched a hedgehog snuffle about on the grass, stopping now and then to scoff down a slug. It stared at us for a moment, then dismissed us and went on its way, disappearing into bushes at the border of the property. Still Vicky and I were silent.

"Stay with me for a few days, but you'll have to report Harry as missing. I'll come with you."

"No, I'll be fine. I'll do it tomorrow. I won't have to pretend to be concerned. I'm so sad, Arthur, but I'm not sorry. I'm not sorry."

I squeezed Vicky tight and her tiny body racked with sobs as she cried her little heart out. She shook and she buried her head in my chest and cried and cried for all the terrible things in the world. For a life lost, for her own life wasted on that man, for her love for him and for her shame for loving such a man. Mostly she cried for her kids.

My phone beeped, it was George. I messaged her back and moments later she appeared around the back, coming through the side gate and down the strip of lawn that ran along this boring semi-detached house. I peeled Vicky off me and said, "Be right back," then went to talk to George.

I filled her in on what had happened, leaving nothing out since we'd left her and Sasha, and she took it well. Not surprising really, as our world was full of this kind of madness. But she was as shocked as I was to find out about Harry, about the man he truly was. Her only concern was for Vicky and the children.

"Can you watch them?"

"Sure. And you're okay? The angel isn't around, is it?"

"I bloody hope not. I've got enough on my plate. But I want this book gone. I need to give it to the vamps. And quick. I can't be having anything dangerous around with the girls here. If anything, and I mean anything, happens, then call me, and Sasha, and just stay put. If you have to, use the portal to come back here, but that's a last resort. Not sure how we'd explain that to the girls. Actually, come on, let's go inside."

George raised an eyebrow but followed me around to the back. She hugged Vicky who was still crying then I left them while I sorted a few things out. I made several trips from the car to the house and took the luggage through the portal and loaded it into the vehicle in the barn, then went out back and told them my plan.

George nodded approval, Vicky just went along with whatever I said. Back inside, George and I each lifted a small sleeping figure carefully in our arms and then we all went through the portal. George would drive everyone back to the house where it was a little safer, well away from the city and its dangers. Sure, the angel could go anywhere, but if I returned to the city it would follow me there, if it was following me. And somehow I just knew there was plenty of other crap sure to make what was already a terrible night even worse.

"Look after them," I said to George. She nodded, then got in the car.

I hugged Vicky and whispered into her ear, "Everything will be all right. You're safe, the girls are safe, that's all that matters."

"Thank you."

I led her to the car, made sure she was buckled in, then opened the barn doors. George drove off, I locked up, then I sat on a straw bale and I cried.

I felt such an overriding sense of sadness and helplessness, and the tears came freely. Those poor fucking kids.

A Plan

My head shot up and I quickly wiped my eyes as the barn door rattled. I sensed nothing malevolent, but I did sense something small and annoying. With a sigh, I got up and unlocked the doors.

"Vicky?"

"I hoped you'd still be here. Have you been crying?"

"Yes." I stared at her, finding it hard to reconcile this woman with the one I knew when we were out working. Here she was, face cleaned up, hair brushed and pulled back into the familiar ponytail, new striped sweater on, looking like a kid's sweetie, boring jeans, and supermarket sneakers. Yet she was a killer, a murderer of bad guys. Fearless, smart, sassy, and utterly fragile.

"Oh. I expected you to say you had something in your eye."

"Real men cry. And they aren't afraid to admit it."

"Er, right. So, um, what's the plan?"

"Vicky, I'm sorry, but I can't get my head around this. Why are you here? Why aren't you with the girls? Why aren't you climbing the bloody walls?"

"I will be if I stay at the house. My mind won't stop, I'm a bag of nerves. I have to do something. I won't sleep tonight, not with all that's happened, with everything I have to do. What am I going to do?"

I thought for a moment, wondered if I should turn her away, send her back to the house, but this was probably for the best. "What you're going to do is come with me to see your brother. We give him the book, and I still haven't told you what happened earlier with him, and then we'll figure out properly what you and the girls will do. Okay?"

"Okay. So, what did happen with Ivan? You still have the book so I guess it didn't go according to plan?"

And just like that we were back being a team of thieves, or one thief, one annoying sidekick. I told Vicky what had happened, about the crap I'd had to deal with, and she listened, only interrupting a few times.

"He's protecting the vampires. Didn't want to take the book with the angel after it like that."

"That's not a reason. If Mikalus wants this book then he knows he'll have to deal with the angel too. He would have known it all along."

"Yes, he would. Or... yes, that's probably it."

"What? What are you on about?"

"It's obvious, isn't it? If Mikalus knew the angel would be after the book, then Ivan knows too, so..."

"So they expect me to deal with it, then hand over the book once there's no risk to them."

"Exactly."

"Fucking vampires."

"Hey, he's family."

"Yeah, and he owes us one. Come on, we need to go see him. He can help sort this out about, er, Harry."

"Bit late to remember his name now," muttered Vicky, but she didn't break down and start crying, she just followed me into the back of the barn and we stepped through the gate, yet again, to the city.

A Walk

Back in the city, I needed a little time to get accustomed to the latest madness. I suggested we go for a wander. Vicky seemed to think it was a good idea too, so we stepped out into the cool night air and walked the streets. Suburbia was a strange place, it felt so nice and gentle, so above-board and wholesome, but we both knew that wasn't the case. That behind the facades of conformity and mass consumerism, the smart lawns, the polished cars, and the colorful hanging baskets, everyone had their own personal demons to fight. Nobody escaped life. Everyone was screwed up.

We walked with a purpose that had no purpose, just us and the cats prowling through the night, the occasional car driving past. The streetlights all worked, casting their sickly yellow glow onto us as we passed beneath, there was no trash, no graffiti, even the trees seemed healthy and happy. All fake, a pretense. Life wasn't like this, the minds of the people that maintained this part of the city weren't like this, and neither were its occupants. Still, it was quiet, nobody tried to mug us, so it was all good.

My mind turned to Cerberus. That was one hell of a mess that was sure to get worse. I regretted Nathan's demise, his replacement sure as shit was no better, and I got the feeling would be a lot worse, but we'd see. I could handle them. Maybe.

I wondered what kind of conversations were going on at their headquarters, what the plan was now Vicky and I knew about the warehouse. I'd always suspected something epic, that over the millennia this secret organization must have amassed a veritable hoard of goodies, but the scale of it was beyond belief.

Would this mean they'd want us gone, and make sure they got what they wanted? Or would they just keep trying to bring me into the fold? Time enough to worry about that tomorrow, for now I had to focus on getting this exchange made then helping Vicky out. I hated to admit it to myself, but part of me resented Vicky for getting me involved in her personal life to such a degree.

I didn't need the hassle, I really didn't. Now I had her and her kids at my place. How long would they stay? Would the girls mess up my kitchen? Of course they would, they were children. Then I felt bad for thinking such thoughts. She was my friend, however annoying she was, and I truly loved her, would do anything for her. But why the hell had she done such a thing? She could have just left him, surely?

Nope, it didn't work like that. Life's never clean and tidy, never simple. She'd been pushed to the edge and rather than fall over she'd fought back in the only way she knew how, making certain once and for all that her family was safe. Now he'd never hurt her, or scare the girls, and she could pick up the pieces and move on. It wouldn't be a fun few weeks or months, that was for sure, as however well she was keeping it together at the moment, she was gonna crash and crash hard once this was over.

On we walked, and then we walked some more. The further we went, the more we got into our stride, keeping up a brisk pace, me having to go fairly slow, Vicky chugging along like a miniature steam train. But it blew away the worst of the nightmares, left us panting and rosy cheeked, and we inhaled the cleaner night air, pollution at an all time low. I felt energized and hyped, Vicky looked the same, but I knew it wouldn't last, that as soon as we stopped, when we collapsed at some point, everything that had happened would come back to her, causing one hell of a meltdown. It would be epic, it would involve a lot of tears, and it would probably involve degrees of wailing and screaming hitherto unheard of. Joy. Couldn't wait.

So I picked up the pace and we found ourselves at the large park the respectable citizens stayed away from at night time. But we weren't respectable, and we weren't citizens. We were gangsters, murderers. We consorted with the scum of the earth and the supernatural entities of the heavens, so we strode in, unconcerned by the dark and the bushes where men could jump us to try to do despicable things.

Ha, let them try. They'd picked the wrong night to try anything on. Part of me almost wanted something like that to happen, for us to be attacked, just so I could unburden myself of the pent-up anger and frustration I felt with pretty much the whole world right now. I knew it was just a sadness, a bone-aching depression waiting to take hold of me. It needed an outlet.

Everything in my world was a lie now. The one thing I thought I could rely on, that gave me hope, was that there were still happy families out there. Sure, I knew Vicky and hubby had issues, and often it seemed like a loveless marriage, but they did right by their kids. All that hope was gone now. He was an abuser and she had killed him. Everything was fucked up, nothing good was left.

My mood was darker than the water of the boating lake as we stood on a small wooden platform, one of many dotted around its edge where fisherman could sit and dangle wire into the water and have a day of peace and quiet as they contemplated their life and caught fish only to throw them back in so they could take their chances then get reeled back in another day. A merry-go-round of freedom and captivity, of gasping for air and then release, only for the inevitable to happen one day and for it to all be over. Just like my life.

I lit up another of Harry's cigarettes, feeling guilty as I knew George would be cross, but I sucked down the smoke then exhaled a cloud over the misty water.

An owl hooted, Vicky cried, and I scowled at life then gave it the finger.

Itchy Leg

The book was giving me grief. It kept wriggling in the pocket of my combats, like a snake trying to escape. The wards weren't holding, the mask that disguised its presence wouldn't stay put, same as before, as it was too damn volatile. Too alien. It didn't belong here, with me. How had the guy who I stole it off kept it hidden for so long? How come the angel hadn't just wreaked havoc and taken it from him? It was hardly protected at all there, so why all this crap now?

Maybe I'd ask Ivan, or Mikalus, or maybe I wouldn't. Honestly, I didn't care. I just wanted it gone, and now seemed like the right time to finally get this over with.

"Come on, it's time to go," I said wearily to Vicky, the high of our walk drained away now, leaving me deflated, exhausted, sad.

"Okay. I'm feeling sleepy, Arthur. I think the walk tired me out."

"Yeah, that will be it," I said, taking her arm as we walked away from the boating lake. I said nothing about it being more likely that the murder of her husband and the stress of thinking about the future would have sent her body into shock, that her system would try to shut down to blank it out. She probably didn't need reminding about any of that.

"Will you look after me?" asked Vicky in a quiet, timid voice.

I stopped at her words, something I'd never expected her to ask. Vicky had always been strong, always shown herself to be resourceful and capable, if annoying, and she must have been very scared to have asked such a thing. She was a proud woman, so this took a lot of guts.

With utter conviction, I looked into the eyes of my friend and I said, "I will care for you, and protect you, in any way I can. I love you, and the girls. You're family. Anything you want, just ask. I may not be the best at reading the signs of women, which is probably why I don't get many dates, so never be afraid to ask. I will protect you and look after you, I swear."

"Thank you." Vicky sagged, like this was what she needed to hear. "But it's not the reason you don't get any dates. It's because you never actually ask."

"Huh?" See, told you I wasn't the best at reading women.

"You're meant to ask. You could have a date tomorrow if you asked rather than tried to be a wise-ass and act clever all the time."

"It's rather soon, don't you think?" I said with a frown.

Vicky smacked me on the arm. "Not me, you idiot. Candy. She likes you."

"Haha, don't be daft. She's utterly gorgeous, never even gives me a hug, and she is way younger than me and absolutely out of my league."

Vicky stared at me for the longest time, and it began to get uncomfortable. "You don't get it do you?"

"Get it? Get what?"

"Let me tell you something about women, Arthur."

"Please. Apparently I have a lot to learn." Was I about to learn the secrets of this most unfathomable of beings?

"There is nothing a woman finds more attractive than a strong man who is gentle at the same time. Actually, there is. Women find men who don't know they are handsome, who are funny without realizing, who are slim and look after themselves, powerful yet humble, and are obviously caring, very attractive."

"Who are we talking about again? I'm none of those things. I try too hard to be funny, I'm not in the best shape, and I kill people. How caring can I be?"

"That's what I'm talking about. You don't realize it, but you're quite a catch. Ask George, she'll tell you. Sasha too."

"George is always telling me I'm not so bad, nice in a rugged kind of way, and that I'm a catch, but she's biased, same as Sasha."

"There you go then. You should ask her."

"Candy?"

"Yes, Candy," said Vicky, exasperated.

"On a date?"

"Yes, on a date. What's wrong with you?"

"Um, life?"

"Well, get over it. Plus, she's really hot."

"I know, right? Those hips, those ti—"

"Stop! I am not having this conversation with you. If you want to get all pervy then save it for other men."

"Sorry, got carried away. So you think I should ask her? What should I say? Where should I suggest we go? What if she says no? If you're winding me up..."

Vicky marched off and shouted, "For a fearless wizard gangster you sure are one hell of a lightweight."

I ran after her and caught her up. She didn't understand. There's nothing scarier in heaven or hell than asking a woman out on a date when she'll probably say no. It dents a guy's pride. Guess it's why I joked around and acted daft. It was a defense mechanism so I couldn't get rejected as I never actually asked, just hinted at sexy times without the risk of being turned down.

My heart fluttered. What a stupid old man I was.

Then Vicky was gone. A black nothingness swept past and up the steep bank leading to the car park.

She screamed. I ran.

What Now?

The blackness spread, losing its density, until I could make out the surreal sight of Vicky flailing in the air moments before the sound of her screams hit my freezing cold ears. Then, just like that, the mist dissipated. Guess the angel could only hold it together for so long like that, or it was playing, having fun with us. Either way, Vicky crashed to the grass at the top of the rise in what I considered to be a most spectacular landing. I took a puff of my cigarette then chased after her.

"Are you okay?" I asked as I hauled her to her feet and looked around in a panic.

"I'm fine, just dirty." Vicky scowled at the mud stains on her knees then squared her shoulders and puffed out her chest.

"That's the spirit. Come on, time to leave."

"You have the book. I want the book."

"So you keep saying," I shouted to the air. "Take it up with the vampires, they own it. I'm just the delivery guy."

"No, you must release it to me. Give it to me."

Again with this crap. Something was stopping the angel just taking what it wanted, and that meant I had an advantage. But how much damage could it do to me, to us? I didn't want to find out. It had destroyed Bones and his crew, although they had it coming, but I doubted the angel knew the difference. Then it struck me, of course it did. Maybe it meant we were the good guys and it would be in trouble if it ended us before our time was officially up. Nonetheless, I grabbed Vicky's arm and marched us away as fast as possible.

The air swirled around us, an impenetrable darkness that contained strong, strange forces. Magic, but not magic as I knew it, as humans know it. I could feel it coalescing, trying to take on substance, but something was interfering with it manifesting as anything solid. Regardless, it warned of danger, and of pain, and I'd had enough of both for a while.

Vicky's ponytail blew, my hat threatened to be swept off my head, and my jacket whipped around me as the wind built until it became an almost tangible barrier to our progress. We marched faster, through the car park, across a street that would soon be bustling with early morning traffic, but the wind followed, dark and nasty, cold and frightful.

It began to nip at us, gaining strength, snapping at our legs and stinging our faces and hands like scorpions lashing out. Soon we were battered and bruised and utterly freaked, but the voice remained silent even as the energy around us grew wilder.

We moved faster, a slow jog at first, then we were running as the stings turned to real pain. Over and over, we both cried out as the nips became strong bites like that of a dog, and I found it hard to believe chunks hadn't been taken from my body. But there were no actual marks, no clothes torn, no flesh broken, just the sensation of being attacked by this darkness that hit like lightning then came at us from a totally different direction, leaving us uncertain which way to turn or what to do next.

And then we slammed into a wall of the stuff right in the middle of a street lined with cars, and houses where the owners slept, maybe even had pleasant dreams. It felt like walking into something pure yet tinged with violence at the same time. A glimpse of an animal innocence mixed with anger and a sense of being in the right, justified in acts of violence because it was for the greater good.

I didn't know how I knew this, could feel this, but it was there, a sense of knowing at least a tiny fraction of this presence that was so far removed from being a human being it may as well have been an alien life form. Which, in many ways, is exactly what it was. I also sensed its regret, that it didn't want to kill us but that it would if it meant it got what it wanted.

And it wanted the book.

But I am a man of honor, even if Ivan had left me to deal with this. I had been paid and I meant to deliver what I'd promised to deliver. Call it old-fashioned pride, call it stupidity, call it whatever you want, but

The Hat delivered. He had a reputation to maintain, and besides, I was annoyed.

Why couldn't I be left alone to steal things in peace?

At the thought, I smiled, then snarled, then shoved back with weary magic nowhere near up to the task of dealing with something like this.

"Fuck you," I said, to an actual, genuine, freaking angel.

It went wild. The blackness intensified, became almost solid, and the outline of something not quite man, not quite anything, just very scary, dare I say intimidating, wavered and flickered then shot right at us, knocking us back, making the tip of the cigarette still in my hand glow fierce orange.

With a growl, then a smile as I noticed it wasn't quite burned down to the filter, I took a final drag then flicked the glowing butt right at the dark form.

Bad idea.

A Bad Habit

"Don't!" screamed Vicky, but it was already too late.

The butt of my delightful cigarette arced through the air gracefully after I flicked it perfectly, spinning end over end like a satellite tumbling through space, but my hands were already sweating as I understood what I'd done.

The tip glowed an angry orange as it burned brighter from its trajectory, and we froze for a split second, knowing what was to come but transfixed by a beacon of light when all around was darkness.

Then time crashed back down on us. We spun on our heels, ran away from my bad habit but both slipped on the potholed asphalt. We stumbled onward and I grabbed Vicky and hauled her in front of me then sprang at her back as the world turned a blinding white. The weight of my stupidity slammed down onto my back just as I landed on Vicky and flattened her onto the road, easily covering and protecting her body with mine.

I expected to be saying a grumpy hello to an unimpressed Death, but, unfortunately, I got no such respite, no escape from the impossible pain that lanced through my back and legs. The stench of my burning flesh stung my nostrils like I'd snorted pig fat.

This was, and I'm not exaggerating, the most stupid thing I'd done in my life so far. Okay, there was the thing with the squirrel, but apart from that.

We'd both read it moments before the cigarette hit the dark form. That it contained immense power and that the cancerous stick was somehow going to play havoc with the energy the angel used to manifest. Magic, or supernatural forces, harness what's already here. It doesn't invent new exotic matter or anything, it uses substance, gas, natural elements to affect the world, and the angel was currently one great big mass of writhing gases and who knew what else. But I hadn't expected it to be quite as epic. Cars were aflame, the combustion caused by the angel's disruption to all that we take for granted, the very air we breathe, had set alight several vehicles in a fireball that engulfed half the street.

I watched, still covering Vicky with my body, as another car caught fire. Knowing what was likely to happen, given my luck so far when dealing with this dude, I ducked just as it exploded. Then another, then another. Car alarms began to wail, Vicky began to wriggle, and I began to moan.

Comes to something when you can't even flick a cigarette butt at an angel without blowing up a damn street.

My back felt achy as hell but I wasn't on fire, hadn't broken anything important, or unimportant either, and was still alive, so it could have been worse. I clambered off Vicky with a lot of moans from her which was just damn ungrateful, and pulled her to her feet. "I think we should go see Ivan. Right now," I said, staring around at the fires, expecting something to come screaming out of the flames being very annoyed.

"Me too."

We scarpered, ran for ten minutes to get away from the scene of the crime as sirens lit up the streets and converged on the chaos. Down a quiet road, I used my wand to unlock a car, started it up, then drove slowly and carefully through the city to get rid of the book, and the damn angel, once and for all.

I swear, we nearly made it, we really did, but my phone rang and I answered it. It was George.

I listened, then said, "Okay," and hung up and glanced at Vicky.

"What? What's wrong? Oh no, it's the girls, isn't it? Are they okay? Have the police found out? Do they want to arrest me?"

I wound the window down, the stench of smoke clinging to our bodies making it hard to breathe, let alone talk. "It's nothing like that, but we have to go home. Now." I dropped down a gear, swerved in the road, then put my foot down and drove as fast as I could.

I was never going to get rid of this damn book.

Back and Forth

"What's happened?" screeched Vicky, the sound piercing my skull like an ice-pick through the ear.

"The girls are freaking out. They woke up and George can't calm them down. They're screaming and shouting and asking where you are. They want to know if their dad is going to take you away, if you've left and they won't see you again. George said they're just scared and out of sorts." It was about as gently as I could put it, when what George had basically said was they were utterly freaked out and crying and screaming and terrified beyond belief their parents had abandoned them. George was really worried, and she had less experience dealing with children than me, so she was at a loss regarding how to handle it without making things worse.

"Those poor children. What have I done, Arthur? What have I done?"

"You did what you thought best," I said, not knowing what else to say. Vicky had done a very, very stupid thing. She had killed their father, right there in the street. I didn't think the girls had seen, didn't think they'd connected the dots, but they could sure as hell come up with any number of wild scenarios of what had happened, even if none were as bad as the truth.

Or maybe they knew, had figured it out, and just couldn't accept it so were losing the plot. Or maybe they really were just scared their dad would come and cart them off, or take Vicky away, and they'd never see their mum again.

See, this is why I was loath to have a partner. I had enough crap to deal with in my own life without headaches like this—at least that's what I tried to convince myself of. People are, when you get right down to it, a bloody nightmare.

But I drove fast, took chances with keeping the location of the gate hidden, and only ditched the car a few streets away, something I would never normally contemplate. Then we ran back, went inside, and hopped straight through the gate.

At the barn, we jumped in a battered Volvo I didn't even remember parking there, then I hammered it through the dark lanes back to my farm with Vicky growing increasingly mental and louder the longer it took.

Outside the farm gate she was out the door before I'd even stopped so I parked up, turned off the engine, and chased after her before she did herself some damage without even getting inside.

I needn't have worried as the security lights were on, highlighting the cobbled courtyard. The front door was open, light spilling out, and George was running around in her Mickey Mouse pajamas chasing after the girls still in their clothes. They screamed and ran madly in all directions, hyper and scared, acting like someone was after them with a large cleaver rather than George sporting Disney night attire.

Vicky was fumbling with the catch to the gate, utterly panicked. I lifted the latch but put a hand to her shoulder before she went off on one. "Just be cool. Don't excite them. Act calm and natural and they'll be fine."

"Arthur, don't try to teach me how to look after my kids. You aren't an expert, you didn't even know you had a daughter, so don't interfere."

"Ouch."

"Sorry, sorry, oh my gosh, I didn't mean that. I'm so sorry."

"It's okay, go get 'em."

I watched as Vicky went to calm her children down. Truth be told, what she said cut pretty deep, hurt more than I'd expected it to. But she wasn't herself, so I understood. Kind of.

Ten minutes later, the girls were inside, Vicky was reading them a story up in the spare room where they were tucked up in a double bed, with a glass of warm milk each, and George and I were in the kitchen.

"You look terrible," she said, handing me a welcome cup of coffee.

"I feel worse."

George sniffed and frowned. "And you've been smoking," she accused.

"I won't ever do it again, those things are dangerous," I muttered. How could she tell over the smell of the smoke from the fires? Faery powers or just suspicion based on past experience? The mysteries of daughters.

"You're giving up?"

"What? No, I meant I'll just have the one here after dinner. Are you nuts?"

"Whatever. So, what's been happening?"

I filled her in on all that had happened, my head spinning so much I wasn't sure if I'd told her what happened after I'd seen her and Sasha earlier, or not. Apparently I had, so there wasn't that much to tell. I left out the bit about me setting the suburbs aflame, figured she'd only tell me off about the smoking again and have the perfect excuse to give me more grief than she already did.

In a panic, my head shot up from where I was admiring the coffee, and I said, "I should go. I've still got the book, so this damn angel will be after it soon enough."

"I don't think so, not here anyway. Sasha and I really beefed up the wards while you were gone. Gotta protect the girls, and us."

"Oh, wow, that's great. Thanks." I reached out with my mind, sending feelers around my house, and sure enough, the place was a fortress. It had been well protected before, but you can't protect against everything or you'd never get in and out yourself. The more I explored, letting the magic talk to me, the more I understood just how adept my daughter was becoming. The new layers of protection had her essence to them, a combination of youthful exuberance and innate patience combined with Sasha's timeless experience and expertise created something unique, and very protective. They'd done a fantastic job. How Sasha knew what to do to guard against angels I had no idea, but she was a resourceful woman and had a lot of knowledge about a lot of things.

"You should go to bed," said George, taking the mug from my hands as it began to slip.

"Can't, too much to do. Gotta go see Ivan."

The next thing I knew, I was lifting my cheek from the cold table, it was light out, the birds were singing, and two excitable children were tugging at my arm saying they were hungry and what was for breakfast?

I rubbed at my face, realized it was six in the morning, and everyone else was asleep, and said, "Don't young people need their sleep?"

"You're so silly, Uncle Arthur," said one of the sprogs, my eyes too unfocused, my ears too blocked, my mind too dulled for me to tell which. "We had a lie-in. What's for breakfast?"

"Yes, we're starving," said the other tiny terror.

Then I was regaled with a chorus of "What's for breakfast?" over and over, as two mini-menaces danced around me full of the joy of youth, the night forgotten, and poor old Uncle Arthur tried to remember where the cereal was as he was befuddled and couldn't think with the kids talking non-stop.

After a little rummaging, I made the girls their breakfast, fixed strong, almost myocardial infarction-inducing coffee—always use medical terms, you'll take it more seriously—and we all sat down. I tried not to freak out about the spilled milk and cereal on the table and we chatted about all the things they could do on the farm while they had a little holiday with us.

Vicky stumbled into the kitchen bleary eyed and yet smiling, obviously for the sake of the kids.

"Oh my God, what have you done?" she squealed before saying good morning.

I shot up, ready to blast. "What? What is it?" I gasped, dripping coffee down my stubble that was fast turning into a beard.

"You gave them Cheerios? Are you mad?"

"It's just cereal," I protested, as the girls wolfed it down eagerly, speeding up before Vicky took it off them. "You traitors," I accused. "You said this was what you always had."

"Haha, gotcha," came the smug chorus of a reply. They both beamed at me and I smiled. Who could stay cross at them?

"Arthur, I told you, they have a healthy breakfast. Nothing full of sugar. Porridge, or granola, something like that."

"What the fu... er, what's granola? Sounds like something you line your driveway with."

Vicky scowled, saying, "You need to get out more."

"I'm always out, that's the problem. Anyway, be my guest." I waved at the kitchen, then realized what I'd done. "Um, never mind. You take it easy. What do you want me to make? You sit down, relax."

Thankfully, she did just that. My nerves weren't up to watching Vicky dismantle my kitchen and spill liquids over every surface.

"It's fine, these two rascals have finished anyway." Vicky smiled at the girls then leaned forward and they all kissed.

"Can we watch TV?" asked the future ruler of the Universe with an evil glint in her eye mirrored by her sister.

"Sure," I said.

They shot off their chairs and ran to the den faster than me knowing I had a date.

Vicky sighed and said, "You really do have a lot to learn about kids."

"Huh?"

"They never watch TV in the morning."

"Why not?"

"Because, er, they just don't. It's bad for them."

I scratched at my wet beard. "Why? If you let them watch it other times, what's the difference?"

"There just is one."

"If you say so. Maybe you've got some things to learn too," I said, smiling.

"Shut up, and make me a coffee."

See, this is the problem with house guests. Bossy as fuck and they mess with your routine. And your kitchen.

Peace

By late morning the house was in disarray. I'd cleaned the kitchen three times then given up, the chickens were fearing for their lives, the pig was fatter than it had ever been, and there was mud in my hallway.

Then, oh bliss upon bliss, everyone left. I said I'd take Vicky to file the report, help her get her story straight, but she said she had it all figured out, knew what to say, and would rather George took her. Guess she wanted female company, which suited me fine. She even sent the Cleaner her money without breaking down, which made me proud.

George said she'd take the girls into town while Vicky went to the police station, and she promised to keep my name out of things, not to say she was staying here, and would give the police her mobile number.

So it was, and I must admit I was greatly relieved, that I had the house to myself. It was quiet, it was peaceful, it was, what did the kids say at this time? Amazeballs? Can I say that? I can't, can I? Oh well.

But the silence and almost instant relaxation were short-lived, for by the time I'd mustered the courage and cleaned the kitchen to a proper standard, and stopped muttering about the many pitfalls of house guests, my mind was whirling and my stress levels were through the roof. What was my problem? Cleaning the fucking kitchen when Cerberus were after my blood, the vampires were waiting for their book, and the damn book was bait for a pissed off angel that had been haunting me since before I'd even stolen the damn thing.

I thought back over the whole sorry mess, standing there with a cloth in my hand in my now sparkling kitchen, and for the first time in a very long time I wasn't sure what to do. Events had finally caught up with me, overwhelmed me maybe, and I was indecisive and unsure of myself. It wasn't like me, but too much had happened, and I'd been going too long with too little sleep. Insomnia is a killer, literally, and it had killed me several times already because I couldn't think straight or act in a rational manner being so damn tired. This was worse. I was beyond sleepy, way past the merely physically tired. I was mentally exhausted, psychically strained, tired right down to my crumbling bones, and running on reserves I didn't have. Even my ears hurt, which was disconcerting. Probably from all the screeching.

It wasn't just the clusterfuck of this job, it was everything else. Life. I was so stressed and so beat up emotionally and mentally because of Vicky and her mess of a life, because I was constantly worried about

George and what she was getting up to with Sasha, and I think for the first time in many, many years I was growing concerned about my happiness and future. Did I even have one?

Basically, I needed a cuddle.

The chat with Vicky about me being rather reticent when it came to asking women out had seemed comical at the time, kind of, but the more I thought about it the more it rang true. I was scared of rejection, scared of having to admit I'd probably always be alone. Nobody to share my bed or my life with. Because, when you got right down to it, who in their right mind would want to spend their life with someone like me?

I stole, I fought, I killed. Not just killed, I murdered. I got into trouble, I mixed with bad company. I had bad habits, like smoking, and I was utterly obsessive. For crying out loud, I was a wizard, and magic users are always one thing above all else. Trouble.

Who would knowingly choose to be a part of that? Probably only someone as screwy as me. I hated to admit it, and had tried my best to never think such thoughts, but it was very likely that I would always be alone. Sure, there had been women, but just short-lived flings spread out over many years. And, of course, George's mother, but that had been a very long time ago. Since then my relationships had either lasted no more than a few weeks or months, or had lasted longer only because I refused to accept what was blindingly obvious. We would never make it.

So I'd given up on women for the most part. I'd had a few encounters, some warmth in the night on occasion, but even that had fizzled once George came into my life. Last thing I wanted was her to meet strange women in the house. She deserved better, something more stable, and I would not introduce her to somebody unless they were very special and I felt like there was a future for us. For all of us.

George may have been fast-approaching true adulthood, but she deserved stability as much as I could offer it, and there wasn't much of it so far. But I did my best, what I knew I could control, and that was to never let her believe she had a new woman in her life unless I was fairly certain it would be permanent.

Unfortunately, I doubted that would ever happen. Here I was, a screwed up, wild wizard in his forties who never slept, who stole and crept out in the night to go do stupid shit, who went home via a magical portal because people were always out to kill him or do something worse to him. Who would want in on that?

Just as Vicky had said, I put up a defensive barrier of joking about and acting the fool to hide my insecurity, to convince myself I didn't need anyone else. That I could look after myself and I was doing just fine, when truthfully I was lonely and scared and wanted to be loved and to love in return. Just like everyone else.

I threw the cold, wet cloth into the sink, snapping out of my reverie, annoyed with myself for letting my mind dwell on such bullshit. What was wrong with me? I was acting like a special snowflake who deserved more than everyone else in the world looking for the same thing. I didn't. If I wanted a partner, someone to share my life with, then I had to try to find that person. This was all on me, my own stupidity and overwhelming fear of failure. I'd beaten down devils and the worst of humanity, I could get a girlfriend if I wanted to.

I could too!

Time enough for that in the future. First I had to get rid of this book, help Vicky through this bad time, try to get George to open up a bit more about what she was up to so I wouldn't worry as much, and maybe, just maybe, get some proper sleep. Not crashing out at my kitchen table. Somehow it never seemed to count, never eased the tiredness.

Sleep, that was it. I should sleep. But what about the book? And the angel? The wards were up, stronger than ever, so maybe that would give us some breathing space. But the angel knew where I lived, didn't it? I wasn't so sure, didn't know how the mind of such a being worked. Did it remember coming here before I even had the book? Was that the actual entity, or was it just a whisper of the future drifting back through time?

I had absolutely no bloody clue, but I knew I was tired, knew the house was quiet, and knew it was now or never as once the women and girls were back, and their number seemed to be growing daily, I wouldn't get a wink of sleep. If I wanted to rest, and boy did I, then I should do it now.

This went beyond needing normal sleep, this was a weariness brought on by stress, and I just wanted it all to be gone. Quiet. A mini-death so I could escape.

Mind made up, at least about one thing, I stumbled like the half-dead creature I was out of my kitchen.

Then I rushed right back in, picked up the cloth from in the sink, folded it neatly, and draped it over the tap so it looked tidy. Then, and only then, did I feel even slightly relaxed.

Time for bed, old man. Alone.

Wow

I didn't even remember going to bed, but I must have walked up the stairs, undressed, and slid under the sweet, sweet covers, as nobody else was there to do it for me. I woke feeling, well, feeling great. And then as I stretched and yawned I felt bad for feeling so good. My world and that of my friends was falling apart and I was smiling and feeling like a new man. That wasn't right.

But hey, why beat myself up about it? It wasn't often I got to feel genuinely rested. In fact, I couldn't remember the last time I had. It was like I'd slipped into the skin of a fresh Hat clone. For a moment, and don't laugh, my heart went nuts as I panicked about the way everything felt, like maybe someone had done something freaky to me and I was in a new body.

One glance down told me all I needed to know. If a secret organization had the ability to create new bodies they sure as shit wouldn't clone mine, they'd use something better. Staring at my hairy legs and knobbly knees told me I was definitely still in my old skin, and I had the wrinkles to prove it.

I stretched out my limbs, making myself as long as possible, easing out knots and tight spots on my body until it was like I'd been put on the rack and everything popped into alignment making my body feel better than it had in years. Maybe it was all the exercise, maybe it was the joy of being alive. Maybe it was giving myself a good talking to and realizing, as I slept, that things weren't actually as bad as I'd convinced myself they were.

I was alive, always a bonus, I had a nice house, lived in a lovely place, had money enough to buy whatever I wanted, but most importantly I had my daughter. Amazingly, I even had a couple of friends. And here's the real crunch, what I'd tried to deny, tried to convince myself was a bad thing, but had somehow come to accept during this wondrous sleep. I loved this shit.

Doing wild stuff, stealing, being hunted, and even doing some hunting of my own, getting up to all kinds of nonsense, learning secrets and uncovering the mysteries of the universe, dabbling in magic and getting to hold the most valuable treasures in existence, even damn Cerberus and their nonsense. I genuinely loved it all.

The Hat had a blessed life, a genuine faery godmother, a beautiful daughter, knowledge and power and got to do things citizens couldn't even dream of. I was one lucky bugger and it was high time I let myself admit that. This was all my own doing. I took full responsibility for my life, and this was what I'd forged through the madness and the mundane dross that it would have been all too easy to let myself sink into. There was no doubt in my mind that I'd achieved something. I'd earned what I had, and what I had was the kind of life I enjoyed, even though much of it was hard and dangerous. I had to accept that I wouldn't have it any other way.

Phew, amazing what a good sleep can do for a guy.

I showered, still smiling, then went up to the attic, sat naked in the middle of the room and entered the Quiet Place where I settled easily into a state of nothingness. Free, I let my spirit soar and absorbed the powers of the cosmos directly into my body and mind until, hours later, and for the first time in a long while, I was genuinely, utterly, completely full of magic.

It's a thing and not a thing, a true energy and yet nothing but the power of the mind. You will magic, nothing more than your own insistence and belief, to come to you, to fill you up, to become it and it you. You become a part of existence itself and can harness the power you absorb. You learn to accept this gift and let it inside, yet at the same time it is nothing of the sort, magic being merely the strength of your character and having the sheer dogged determination to use it. To believe in its existence and be utterly certain that what you wish of it will become a reality.

Faith. It all comes down to faith. Are you a believer or not? If you are, if you are convinced of the existence of this primordial force as much as you are of your own, then you can use magic, because it is yours, and you have that right.

But, you still have to let it inside, to focus like most can't even begin to understand. To be quiet and still and empty and accepting, and I was all of these things because I was none of them. I was empty and by being empty I became full, and if that sounds like religious mumbo-jumbo, eastern philosophy mixed with a belief in mind over matter, then so be it. Because, when you got right down to it, this is what worked and that's all there is to it.

Everyone has their own way of wielding magic, and sure, there are items, words, and marks that all have power, but it all comes from the mind, all starts and ends there. And as I uncrossed my stiff, hairy legs, and stood naked in an empty room at the top of my house, I was fucking dangerous.

And smiling.

Then the front door banged open and shit got serious again.

Here We Go

With a sigh, yet still feeling uncharacteristically positive, so upbeat in fact that I wondered if I'd somehow ingested something I aught not to, I went and got dressed. Vicky and the girls, and George, were home. My peace was shattered, my kitchen was undoubtedly already messy, and reality had definitely come crashing in, probably through the window, like a brick.

But it was with a light step and a happy heart that I wandered downstairs into my kitchen, smiling like a lobotomized wizard with a big wand in his pocket. Happy days.

"What are you grinning at?" asked Vicky with a scowl as she bustled about at the sink while the girls blew chocolate milk at each other through straws. You'd have been proud of me, I didn't even run for a cloth or anything, although I did keep glancing at the one by the sink.

"Yeah, you look guilty," said George, pulling off her high heels and rubbing her feet. Damn, the untidiness was catching. We had a strict rule about shoes off in the hall, or at least never wearing them in the kitchen.

"What? Just feeling good. Happy. Hey, kids, have you had a nice day with Aunty George?"

"Great. We went everywhere."

"Can we go again tomorrow, Aunty George? Can we, can we?"

"Ugh, we'll see," said George, looking exhausted.

"How did it go?" I asked Vicky, and boy did I wish I hadn't.

For the next hour, while the girls ran around, went to play, rushed back in who knows how many times, and finally settled into shouting at the TV in the other room, I was regaled with tales of woe and police ineptitude, plus stories about the girls running riot in shopping centers by George. I learned several very important facts though. One, taking two excitable children shopping is definitely not something I will ever do. And two, telling the police that your husband is missing and that you think he's run off takes many hours and mostly involves hanging around in cold waiting rooms, filling out a lot of forms, and that busy, stressed-out police officers have better things to do with their time than care. The fact they had to make a round-trip that lasted hours because they couldn't just go through the portal didn't help matters either.

"So that's good, right?" I asked, traces of contentment still lingering even though the hour had done a good job of sucking the life out of me.

"Suppose. They didn't seem like they were suddenly going to begin investigating his disappearance and suspect me of you know what."

"There you go then. Trust me, if you go back every few days, or call them and say you're worried and he's still missing, they'll look into it a bit. But once, er, once certain things are found, then it'll all be over." I was watching my words because I was paranoid the girls might come in, but I needn't have worried, they were engrossed in their show.

"This is so terrible. What have I done? What about the girls?" Vicky broke down, and judging by the look George gave me this certainly wasn't the first time it had happened while they were out.

"They're young, they're strong like their mum, so they will be fine. Besides, you said they were scared of him. They told you. You just have to make sure you tell them the right thing, that Daddy had an accident which is what he has had, totaled his car, probably be found in a few days. They'll get over it, same as you will. Right? Right?"

"Right," said Vicky.

"You understand what I'm telling you? It's all taken care of. He had an accident. He crashed his car. Give it a few days and then you can grieve and go to his funeral and then get on with life."

Vicky burst out crying.

"Dad!"

"What? What did I say?"

Sometimes, make that all the time, I really don't understand women. I didn't back then, I don't now, and I never will.

She was the one who killed him, why was she getting upset about his bloody funeral? Because they'd shared a life together, that was why. That she loved him and hated him and more than anything wanted the life she'd pretended she had. Now it was over. For ever. Gone. She had killed her husband and I think it was only now it was sinking in, the repercussions becoming a reality.

"Sorry, I was being insensitive. Today took a lot out of you, you were brave, very brave. Go lie down, have a rest, we'll watch the girls."

Vicky looked absolutely awful. Eyes sunken, dark bags underneath, hair sticking out, and when she stood I had to catch her or she'd have fallen over. I said nothing, but she felt bony and I knew this level of stress would be playing havoc with her. She stumbled off upstairs without a word, without even telling the girls. She really was out of it to be that remiss.

George and I spoke for a while as we prepared dinner, something simple but hearty so everyone would tuck in, and we both agreed on one thing. Vicky should rest and she was to be made to eat no matter what. I knew her, and she would run until she collapsed, would forget to eat, focusing solely on the girls, and then everything would spiral out of control. I'd seen it before, it was happening now, so she had to take it easy.

The girls came in later and moaned about the Buster Keaton short I was watching, then, after a while, they began to laugh, and to ask about the show, and then we were all laughing, even George, who usually just rolled her eyes at his antics. For the first time in what felt like years, and had maybe never happened, the kitchen was filled with genuine laughter, young and old and in-between.

Everyone forgot about the world outside and even Vicky, when she surfaced, looking a little better for a nap, laughed a little. Maybe at the show, or maybe because she was so relieved that her girls were happy.

It was the oddest thing, but we had a nice dinner. Vicky ate everything put on her plate, the girls chattered about things that were entirely alien to me, music and friends and fashion and new ways of talking to their friends that didn't involve actually picking up a phone and speaking, and then before we knew it they were in bed.

Soon, the kitchen was clean, and the three adults sat around drinking coffee, talking about this and that, keeping conversation light. Why? Because we had so much serious stuff to talk about and do that nobody wanted to go there as we knew the mood would darken and none of us wanted that darkness.

For a while we just wanted to be content with each others' company and lock out the madness that waited just outside the door.

Alone and Dangerous

George had plans and I told her not to change them. She was a good girl and was more than willing to stay home to look after Vicky and the girls, but I wanted her to carry on with her life, not get caught up in our mess. Vicky was obviously beat, and didn't even insist on coming out with me. Besides, she couldn't, as she had to look after her children and nothing would make her leave them alone.

After George left, I gathered my wits—the hardest thing to find—then got my gear together, which mostly consisted of ensuring I had the book, my hat, my wand, and putting on a jacket. I promised Vicky life would return to normal soon, or a new normal anyway, and that we were sure to have lots of wild new adventures.

I also insisted that under no circumstance was she to open the door to anyone, or anything. I was paranoid, but rightfully so. The wards were there to protect her, nothing could get past them, but she was not to invite anyone in, that way lay disaster. As long as she stuck to those rules she'd be fine and the girls were in the safest place possible. She agreed, I left.

Rather than drive to the barn and go directly to the city and meet with the friendly local vampires, I decided to take advantage of my good mood and go for a walk. Mousehole, the local village, was an astonishing place but I hadn't spent much time there lately, having been preoccupied with this and that as is the way for us wizards, and I missed it. I missed the harbor, the steep hills, the tiny fisherman's cottages, the peace and the feeling of timelessness that settled over the place when it wasn't tourist season.

All the sightseers and holiday makers were long gone now, just the locals left. They'd all be tucked up in their beds, sleeping soundly, nothing but the crash of distant waves, the screeching of gulls, the water lapping against the harbor walls, the creak of boats both ancient and new, and that rarest of things, the sound of nothingness. No sirens wailed here, no air pollution, just a brisk sea breeze that calmed the spirit and settled the mind.

I almost ached for such solitude and peace, so I drove to the heart of the village, parked up in a side street, stepped out onto the ancient cobbles and felt instantly at home.

It truly was a beautiful place, unspoiled even after years of heavy tourism, much like the rest of Cornwall. It kept its integrity and spirit intact, and although more than half the houses were owned by weekenders, and the locals could hardly afford to rent let alone buy, it somehow still held many families that had made it their home for generations. Of course, it would all change for the worse over time, but right now, right here, and in this moment, it was still a quaint, ancient, perfect fishing village. Quiet, proud, and accepting. Just like the locals.

I wandered lazily down to the harbor, feeling the salt sting my eyes and the wind bite my cheeks, rejoicing in nature's gift. Searing away the last vestiges of manic aggression and anger I felt, scouring me clean and wholesome only for a while. Boats bobbed on the still water at the harbor and I stepped right up to the edge, let my feet inch over the paving that dropped down into the water, and stared into the black depths, seeing nothing but the reflection of the few street lights I knew switched off soon.

At that thought they did switch off, and the village became dark, just a few small lights dotted about the harbor stopping it from being pitch black. As my eyes grew accustomed to the gloom, I made out the shapes of boats and the piles of fishing gear dotted around the harbor ready for the morning. I smelled fish and salt, sand and water, nothing more.

My footsteps echoed around the harbor as I wandered with no end in mind, just walking to enjoy the ambiance and soak up the peace and energy only water and hundreds of years of honest human work can provide.

Finally, I settled up on one of the high walls that stopped the worst of the weather from encroaching and ensured the harbor waters were still, defenses that fought harder every year to protect the coastline. I dangled my legs over the edge, facing the sea. I listened to lone gulls far away as they screeched, refusing to sleep for whatever reason, and let the sound of the waves fill my mind until it became a meditation of sorts.

This was real life, this was the truth of the world. All our stupid games and the crap we did, all our worries and stresses, our pre-occupations and our obsession with minutiae, it meant nothing in the grand scheme of things. I was a little man on a little wall in a little village in a little country in a world where there was more water than land in a universe where nearly everything was emptiness. Kind of puts things into perspective.

So it was with much regret that I swung my legs over the wall, adjusted my hat, brushed my hair from my eyes, turned my attention from inward to out, and stood with a sigh.

I turned my back on the vastness and the peace, faced back toward the village, and traced the movements of the foggy shape as it darted from one tenebrous space to the next. It was ephemeral and kept flickering as if trying to find a solidity, huge then small, animal then human then nothing of the sort. Jagged then smooth, black as the harbor water then nothing but a whisper.

All the while, strange slivers of sound came to my ears. Wails and pleas, threats and promises, words that were no words and emotions beyond my grasp. Needs so deep I failed to grasp their true importance, desire so strong that it reached out and almost strangled me.

I walked toward this assault, knowing the time had come. That here, in a tiny fishing village on the edge of the country, I was to finally come face to face with an angel straight from a heaven I didn't believe in. And do battle.

Feathers

The shrouded mass darted this way and that, knocking over lobster pots, pulling over large frames holding fishing nets, and generally acting crazed. Hell, it even dragged an anchor and chain around as it spasmed in a frenzy, as though it couldn't quite get a grip on this reality. I stopped and waited, unafraid, past that now, just wanting this to be resolved so I could go home and put my feet up and watch Buster Keaton until I wore out the discs.

I spun as the shade shot up onto the high defensive wall, and was confronted with a spreading soot that stretched out then began to coalesce.

"Make your bloody mind up," I muttered.

I had to hand it to the guy, he knew how to make a dramatic appearance. Small lightless feathers fell from nowhere all around. I held out my calloused hand, steady as a rock, and let a fluffy feather like that of a newborn chick settle in my palm as before. I blew it and it sailed off, then came to rest on the water.

Mesmerized, I watched the angel consolidate, drawing power from somewhere until there was a faint outline of something humanoid. Then the air crackled and energy from the heavens shot down like black lightning, and the angel screamed. Midnight shards of ephemeral strangeness careened off in all directions, the feathers fell like rain until there were enough to make a lovely eiderdown duvet, and the semi-figure curled up on itself until all I could make out was an amorphous blob.

Lightning cracked the sky again, dark as the depths of the deepest ocean, but it was edged with silver this time, and it lit up the harbor until it was like day, everything luminous. Blinded, I covered my eyes, praying it hadn't done permanent damage, but moments later all was drab again and I removed my hand cautiously.

The air had taken on a lightness, as if imbued with something holy, as though the angel had called down heavenly light to dispel the emptiness. It was a twilight, that moment before day and night when the world becomes almost monochrome, when the sun has set yet it isn't quite dark. Up on the high harbor wall, fifteen feet above me, I watched the angel unfurl. It was a solid presence now. Dense, foreboding, powerful. The silver light remained, outlining every part of the angel as it stood.

A man stood above me, large and muscular, one of those annoying figures you see in magazines, all paper-thin skin and six pack abs. Plates of steel for a chest and shoulders so wide you want to hack them off and tell the dude to get a normal body like everyone else. He was handsome, somehow managing to be slender yet well-muscled, a body that made me dislike him even more. Even his bloody thighs were chiseled, a teardrop for a quadriceps—he probably had muscles on his toes. Yet at the same time he managed to look streamlined and in proportion, probably because the muscle wasn't excessive, was just an illusion because of his ultra-low body fat.

He was also tall, six two maybe, with a handsome face and impossibly straight hair that hung down like a black sheet on a washing line when there's no wind. He raised his head but most of him was in shadow, nothing to do with the light. He created his own, was more shadow than not, so I couldn't see his features or too much definition as he inched forward. Thankfully, that included angel penis, as I really wasn't in the mood for such things, and it would feel dirty even to me to be staring at such an appendage. If it was on show I knew I'd have to look, just to say I'd seen one.

He lifted his arms out to the side, continuing the drama, and then his wings sprang out behind the silhouette of a cross. Huge, slender, perfect wings in proportion to his body unfurled with a grace no human could ever have, and then they snapped into position, each feather divine, splayed at the edges like long, sensual fingers.

This creature wasn't just black like we think of it as color, he was darkness itself. As though he sucked in the light and made it his own. He created shadow. It writhed across his body and now and then reached out for something solid and slithered about at his feet, crawled down the wall of the harbor with inquisitive tendrils as if searching for something.

Not something. Me. I didn't know what this was, this shadow, but I knew I didn't want it anywhere near me, that its touch would not be good, that he controlled it and could use it like rope to bind me. Call it intuition, call it paranoia, but I took several steps back and whistled up at the dude now his entrance had been made.

"Very impressive," I shouted. "You gonna lay an egg next?"

"You have what is mine," he said, the voice gentle but full of malice. A warning. No more games.

"It belongs to somebody else now. I'm just the delivery guy. You'll have to wait, take it up with him when he takes possession."

"I must have it. You will give it to me." His wings ruffled and angled upward. Was he going to launch? Fly above me and drop angel poop on my hat?

"Look, buster, we've been through this. I don't own it, it isn't mine to give. Can't we talk about this, come to an agreement without all this bloody nonsense? What's so important about it anyway?" I figured I may as well ask as nobody else had told me a damn thing about this bloody book, and I had a good mind to just throw it into the water and be done with the whole sorry mess. Although I assumed the angel would have something to say about that.

"You foolish child. You know nothing of the things you steal. You are consumed by greed, care nothing for the truth."

"So, enlighten me."

"Enough. I have not come to discuss such matters. We. Are. Done."

That sounded pretty final to me, and besides, I was becoming cold, so thought maybe going home and sitting by a radiator in my nice clean kitchen without any freaky dudes waving their feathers at me sounded nice right about now. I backpedaled, keeping my eyes on this creature, wishing I knew more about angels and more about this one in particular.

What was his name? Where had he come from? What could he actually do to me? I thought back to my musings after he'd destroyed Bones and his crew, and decided I must have been right. If I didn't have hate in my heart, didn't try to destroy him, maybe he had to abide by the same set of rules? Damn angels, way too complicated.

I dared not turn my back on him though, because this was all conjecture, and the truth was I didn't know what he was capable of. Nobody I knew had ever met an angel before. You couldn't summon them, couldn't draw a circle, call their name, and make them appear like you could with many of the demon sub-genres. Angels were different, and angels were far more dangerous than most demons. But it was all from stories. I'd never been told of a genuine encounter before, just read about them or heard second-hand tales passed down from master to pupil. And you know what the old guys are like with their tales. They love to embellish, freak out their pupils.

But what mainly concerned me was what kind of angel was this? One from up there, or one from down below? Not in the physical sense, heaven and hell, as the afterlives and the eternities that exist don't work like that, it's much more complicated, but you still had what I guess you can call the holy and the damned. Those who felt nothing but disdain for humanity, and those who sympathized with us poor fools suffering down here on our rock hurtling through space towards its destruction.

But it was still pretty insignificant to them. They came from places where the struggles of humanity were more of an abstract concept than anything they related to. Their lives, their immortality, their existence was like comparing that of an ant to a spaceman. They had a whole different perspective on things. This I knew from what I'd learned, but I could also sense it, feel it, knew it to be true just by being in his presence.

He saw all of this as troubling, an inconvenience, and he was definitely pissed, but on the scale of things, on the scale of his immortal life, it wasn't like it mattered to him that much. Yet, at the same time it did, and this was what confused me. He wanted this book very badly, yet I sensed this was a brief distraction, something that would be entirely forgotten once finished with. I suppose if you live forever, have been about since before man even knew he was a man, and would be around long after humanity ceased to exist, then dealing with cocky wizards isn't something that holds much weight.

Well, it meant plenty to me, and until I knew more about this guy I was going to do everything I could to stay away from him.

So, brimming with magic, something I knew he respected, I opened my mind to the vastness, focused my will, and I disappeared.

Yeah, that's right, The Hat has mad skills when he's on form.

Goddamn

"Ugh, fuck, fuck, fuck." Something went seriously wonky and I felt my body melting like I was turning into water. I was over-confident, figured I could bring up an old spell, that muscle memory, okay, wizard memory, would ensure that it worked flawlessly. But it hadn't, and I was lying flat on the ground with my face pressed into something fishy that had been trodden on by who knew how many people.

My limbs felt heavy, weighed down with magic that had not done what I wanted it to, which was my own fault for trying something not done for years. Making yourself invisible is no easy thing, especially when you're dressed, and I should have known better. I could have easily brought up a forcefield, or even sunk through the earth itself and hidden, but that underground stuff always freaked me out and I get claustrophobic. It served me right for trying to be a smart-ass.

I clambered to my feet, feeling pretty damn stupid, just in time to witness something truly beautiful.

The angel lifted his wings, they flapped gently, causing the air to ripple and a gentle breeze to tickle my face, the sound melodic, and then he launched from the wall and glided down. He landed in front of me.

"Damn, but you're impressive up close," I said with a wistful sigh, deciding right there and then to visit Beast more often.

"I am an angel," he said, confused by my admiration, as if it would be taken for granted.

"Yeah, I can see that." I got a glimpse of angel private parts, and now that image is stuck with me forever. I hated him even more.

"The book." He held out a hand as his wings acted independently and folded back and behind him. Their tips reached past his head, like horns protruding from his back, making him devilish and a little intimidating.

"Sorry, no can do."

"So be it." This heavenly body, this shaded angel of annoyance, he lost his appeal then. His handsome features contorted into a snarl of rage so base, so full of anger and annoyance that it was like he'd torn a mask off. Muscles spasmed and his nostrils flared as his eyes shone with silver pinpricks. His lips twisted and he snarled like a wild animal as the long, manicured nails on his hands sliced at my face without warning.

I staggered back, hand going to the deep welts he'd gouged across my cheek and nose, almost taking out an eye. Fuck, he was going to kill me. So much for not being able to lay a hand on me. Guess I'd got that wrong and he'd just been playing mister nice guy.

As blood dripped, so my anger surged, and my wand was out of my pocket and blasting before I had chance to consider my actions. He dodged a wild arc of bright energy that would have incinerated a human and as he did so I noticed that his nails were steaming. I paused, waiting to see what he'd do, and he cradled his hand as the steam grew thick like he was burning from the inside out.

"You can't hurt me, can you? It does something to you, takes too much out of you. What, there a law or something? No harming humans that don't want to kill you?"

"It's mine," he hissed, letting his arm drop. The nails fell silently to the ground, and new ones, just as shiny and perfect as the old, slowly grew from his fingers. What the hell was this, Hat vs Wolverine?

"Sorry, buddy, but try again another day. Maybe if you told me what this is really about, what the book contains, why you need it, I might reconsider. But otherwise..." I shrugged, figured now was as good a time as any to get out of there, so, putting many years of on-off practice in action, I ran away.

I got to the car and drove quickly to the main road out of the village, trying to get a handle on all this, what it meant and what I should do. I felt sorry for the guy, understood enough to know there was a lot I should know but didn't, and had half a mind to go back and give him the book. But something stopped me, some piece of knowledge niggling at the back of my mind that told me that would be a very, very bad idea.

This was an angel, and they were sneaky buggers, and they never let you see their true selves. Sure, they could manifest as something we recognized, given the right circumstances, but what you saw was definitely not what you got. Not what they really were. Just the closest thing they could come up with that you'd understand.

This was a creature born of the powers of creation, forged in a time when all was roiling energy, when magic and reality mixed, when demons and all the many creatures of the Nolands came into being. When fae and elves and all the rest burst into existence in the other places. Humanity came last, the leftovers, a poor cousin to the rich tapestry of immortal existence other races were graced with.

And I felt sorry for him? Screw him. I had a code of honor I lived and sometimes died by, and I'd been paid. I had to deliver.

Right then I made up my mind, threw indecision out of the window. No more playing with angels or feeling sorry for beings that had until the end of time to get over any slight I might inflict. This was my world, my life, my here and now, and I had to abide by my own set of rules, however imperfect they might be.

Then the bugger slammed onto my windscreen and I drove off the road and hit a tree.

Grrr.

You Wanna Piece?

I ripped my seatbelt off, my anger rising. What was with this guy? What did he think he could do? If he'd just talk rationally, explain, then maybe things would be different, but no way was I going to give him the book now.

I tore open the door, slid on the bank of the ditch, and sighed as the crumpled car hissed and steamed. Great, now I'd have to walk.

Maybe not.

A ton of bricks landed on my shoulders and I slammed into the mud, slid down the embankment, and got a face full of fetid water. I grew livid as the weight on my back increased and shoved me harder into the sludge. I felt it rip at my clothes, searching for the book, the pressure on me increasing, warning me in no uncertain terms that I was no match.

And then I laughed, and my shoulders shook with mirth, and the load lightened. I reached out a bruised arm and fumbled about for my wand, then smiled as I gripped the warm wood. I shunted will into the wood and a fat cushion of air inflated underneath me like an invisible ball, springing me and my passenger away from the ground.

We whacked against the car, me not feeling a thing as it was him that hit, and then I hurtled forward, straight back into the dirt. Clambering to my feet, I whipped about only to find him staring at me, his shoulders already sagging, his face back to just annoyingly handsome rather than feral.

"You're a feeder, right?" He said nothing, just stared, but I understood then. "You can only become a solid form if there's enough emotion. What, you need anger, or fear to became solid, but you need something more to actually try to interfere in the physical world? You need my own violence to hurt me. Well, tough luck, buddy. There isn't much that scares me, not much at all, and I don't want to hurt you. So take a hike. That's what I'm going to do."

And with that I just walked away. Partly because I was still a little scared, and wasn't sure I was quite correct in my thoughts. But I felt that somehow he was feeding on emotions and the less concerned I was about him, the less he could do to me.

I didn't turn at the pitiful wailing, but looked skyward as I felt a strong breeze tug at my hat, almost lifting it off my head. I scraped dirt from my eyes, cursing as I felt the deep slices in my face, and saw wisps of darkness dissipate as the angel sped away, losing solidity, until it was nothing, gone.

With no other choice, as I didn't want to steal a car as it would mean walking all the way back to the village and I was halfway home anyway, I wiped myself down, patted the pocket still containing the book, and marched up the hill feeling a little sorry for myself. I had more questions than answers, but knew I had to find out, just for my own peace of mind.

Half an hour later, bedraggled, face burning, no amount of magic seeming to heal the damaged flesh, and with infection worrying me, I unlocked my front door and took off my boots. The house was silent, the hour was late, but I had unfinished business. This time there'd be no dawdling, I'd do what I had to do and get answers at the same time.

So I got cleaned up, changed clothes, focused on the welts as I stared in the mirror until they mostly healed over, and was back out the door in ten minutes.

Time to go meet some vampires.

That Tingly Feeling

I couldn't shake the feeling that I was being followed. Probably because I was. Now the angel had a fix on me, it seemed it wasn't going to leave me alone. It didn't interfere, did nothing at all in fact, and it wasn't as though I could see it. But I knew it was there, following George's Mini Cooper as I drove to the barn. How the hell did she fit in this thing? My legs were squashed up by the steering wheel, there wasn't enough head-height to wear my hat, and I generally felt ridiculous, as though I was driving Noddy's car.

But it was nippy, got me there super-fast, and just as well. My nerves were frayed. I didn't know what I was dealing with any longer as my assumptions were clearly mistaken, and I had the terrible suspicion this was far from over. I needed information, but was in no mood to go waking people up who could offer me some insight into this.

I closed the barn and performed a familiar ritual. Through the gate, into the kitchen in my city house, check the wards, out the front door, walk a few streets, get into yet another car, never quite sure if it was one of mine or not as they changed so fast, then off I drove, feeling almost like I was floating through the sleeping city, buoyed yet increasingly worried by the whole debacle. I didn't like encounters with things I didn't understand, and this angel, this feeder, was concerning me.

Regardless, I made a call to Ivan. Judging by the way he answered so fast, he'd been waiting for it. He said to come to his new place, and gave me the address. Very swanky. I knew he'd moved but hadn't been there, just got regaled with stories of how amazing it was from Vicky.

Fifteen minutes later, I was at the entrance to an exclusive building where a doorman nodded at me, smiled, and let me in. Guess I was expected. I knew instantly that the rumors were true, that this was no normal upmarket apartment building. This was gangster territory, Ivan's territory, plus vampires. Lots, and lots, of vampires.

They'd kept a low profile, even lower than normal, since their old place burned down and Mikalus had been resurrected. They'd simultaneously upped their game, taken a tighter grip on their businesses, expanded and increased their holdings, partly because of Mikalus' influence, but also because Ivan was one seriously smart dude. I knew he was deeply entrenched in the life and culture now, but they'd also become even more secretive than ever, with hardly a whisper about them even in the magical community as nobody knew what they were up to beyond wild speculation or little pieces of information it was tough to believe were true.

But as I passed people in the lobby, checking mail in the rows of gleaming boxes, as others came and went from the spacious elevators, and doors opened and closed as I took the stairs and wandered the halls slowly on my way up, just to get an idea of what this place was, it became evident this was a building occupied by vampires. Important vampires, gangsters, bodyguards, and many familiar faces I knew helped Ivan run his business.

I was in a gangster/vampire den, and that was no place to be.

Finally, I made it, puffing and panting, to the eighth floor. Ivan obviously didn't get the penthouse on level nine, and that made me wonder. How did we know so little about them all? It had always been like this. They were secretive beyond belief, more than Cerberus, so little known about how it all worked, let alone what they all did, the extent of their power, that often they were dismissed as not even bit players on the supernatural scene. Yet we all knew they had immense influence before, and who knew how much now Mikalus was back running the whole shebang, with Ivan doing a fab job of improving their finances and their grip on the underground?

Down a plush red carpet, with potted plants next to the apartment doors, and expensive paintings on the walls, I finally came to the last door. Two large bodyguards stood to attention outside. Alert, pale, violent. Vampires. I nodded to them, they did likewise, then one knocked.

The door opened moments later, there was a brief conversation while I was held to the side, then I was ushered in with a sweep of a meaty hand.

"Fucking hell, Ivan, this place is a palace."

Ivan, dressed in a black silk dressing gown, making him look like a pencil, frowned at the room, or series of rooms as far as I could tell through the arches that led off to even more luxury, and said, "It's what is expected. Where I meet some of the more self-deluded bosses, and what the First feels is befitting my position."

He clearly didn't like it, and it was understandable. Ivan came from nothing, had lived down amongst the lowlifes, worked for his old boss for years in seedy dives, hands-on and immersed in street-level life, this was a whole other ballgame.

"You've definitely come up in the world." I took in the lavish furniture, the impressive rugs, the lamps and the designer sofa, the expensive paintings, the rich drapes, even the bloody light switches looked like they cost more than my kitchen.

And, oh, the kitchen. I wandered over without being given permission, ran my hand across the cold marble counters, lusted over the double oven set up, gasped when I saw the sink tap, something I knew cost thousands, and the coffee maker would make any barista drool.

"This is fucking ace."

Ivan came over and scowled at the kitchen. "I hate it. I don't even cook. I just use the microwave. I'm moving, and soon."

"Guess it's down to what you like. Why'd you move here if it's not your thing?" I asked, intrigued despite how keen I was to get business done and to leave.

"Mikalus needed me, needed us all close. The Second, the true Second, he wanted everyone together. Safety in numbers I guess." Ivan shrugged then wandered off into a bedroom. I got a glimpse of silk sheets and a bed larger than most apartments before he closed the door. It snicked closed with perfect engineering. I could open and close a door like that all day. There was something immensely satisfying about it.

While he was gone, I occupied myself with exploring what turned out to be mostly empty cupboards, just to watch the doors close softly. I admired the cutlery drawer and felt envy when I found a stack of designer tea towels. But it was all too clinical even for me. Ivan wasn't lying when he said he hardly used the kitchen. Everything was brand new, most of it never used.

Like me, he came from the streets, where the world had a tarnish and was rough around the edges. Sure, I liked nice things, especially the kitchen, and Ivan liked smart, tailored clothes, but you had to keep it real, be true to yourself. He looked more at home, certainly more at ease, in his small office in the factory than he did in what was meant to be his home, somewhere to relax and be himself.

Ivan emerged wearing a smart but casual dark blue suit, no tie, and joined me at the kitchen counter which I was stroking lovingly.

"Sorry about leaving you. I have responsibilities. People depend on me, and Mikalus needs me."

"No problem. I was pissed, but I get it. You're a bigwig now, more valuable than lowlife wizard thieves."

"Don't sell yourself short, Arthur. You're the best at what you do."

I turned and studied him. He looked preoccupied, almost haggard. "I'm not selling myself short. I know who I am, what I am. I understand the game and how it works. That there's always a boss. Do you?"

Ivan sighed, his shoulders sank, and he nodded. "I do. This is a trying business I find myself in. Being the boss of so much of this dark world is exhausting. Do you know how much scum there is in our world? I wasn't aware of just how despicable so many of the criminals truly are. Now I know."

"Now you know," I said with a nod. "Anyway, to business. Yours, I believe. Now we're done, and it's your problem. And it's a massive one. Problem that is." I pulled out the book, slapped it down on the marble, and made to leave.

I felt instantly lighter. Ivan and the vampires could deal with the bloody angel now, it was no longer my problem. And good riddance. Basically, I was annoyed at him because I had to be annoyed at someone.

I got halfway to the door before Ivan stopped me. "Don't you want to know what's inside?"

"No!" I turned, but it was too late. Ivan pulled the small black book from the plastic baggy, and flipped it open.

"You fucking dipshit."

Blame Me

It was my own fault. I should never have taken the wards down until I was at the door, preferably the other side of it. Maybe the door to the building. But I'd lifted them when I handed it over, thinking it best to remove anything that linked me to the book. This was what the angel wanted, not me. I'd just assumed, foolishly, that it would take a while for the angel to home in on its property.

What I hadn't taken into consideration was that Ivan wasn't that involved with magical items and to him it was all rather novel. Plus, he'd obviously forgotten he used to go by the name Brains, as he'd clearly left them far, far away.

"Are you nuts?" I shouted, running back and slamming my hand over his, closing the pages.

We looked at each other, him in shock, me with worry, and I knew we both felt it. The power contained within the black pages. The glimpse of the spidery white writing, written by a practiced hand in scratchy script with embellishments on the page I saw, in a language I neither understood nor cared to, was enough to do something to us, to the room, maybe to the world as a whole.

This was heady stuff, powerful. Words with meaning, words with power, a tome of incredible potency.

"I just wanted to see what all the trouble had been about. Don't worry, the building is well protected. We have wards too, Arthur, put in place by the best practitioners in the world. You may not know it, but some vampires are adepts too."

"Yeah, well, that's great news and I'll file it away in the drawer labeled stuff I never knew about vampires until someone did something really fucking stupid, but there's a rule about weird-ass magical books belonging to angels. And the rule is, you let some other twat open them."

"Did you see it?" Ivan had a familiar gleam in his eye. I'd seen it before, on many faces, and when I looked in the mirror sometimes, and it always meant one thing. Trouble.

I took a deep breath then sighed. I should get out of here. Whatever Ivan thought, however well the place was protected, the angel would be on the trail now. Better make this quick.

"Let me give you a piece of advice," I began, putting my hand over Ivan's as his fingers walked unconsciously toward the book. "Don't get caught up in the power of objects you don't understand. It's one thing looking at a magical book for spells or to tell you certain things, if, and I mean if, you know what the book contains, but even then they're prone to surprise you. Like, you turn a page and the words crumble to the edges and then leap out at you and try to bite your face off. What you don't do, ever, is open something without knowing at least what to expect. Do you know what this book is?"

"No idea. I just had to get it. For Mikalus."

"Right. And we aren't Mikalus. He's the original fucking vampire. He's been resurrected from his own ashes by the blood of his chosen ones, and you. He isn't a regular guy. Me and you, and yes, I'm a wizard with extra lives and you're a new vampire that can shape shift, we're just regular dudes in comparison. This book belongs to an angel, and I just had a run-in with it. It's dangerous, very serious about getting this back. And you opened the book. It'll be pissed. Leave it to Mikalus and the angel. My advice? Give it to him as soon as possible. Like, right now."

"That's very good advice."

We turned at the soft, yet at the same time gravelly, voice. Mikalus.

Like my night wasn't bad enough already.

Telling Tales

"I see you opened the book," said Mikalus, nodding at the tiny tome like we weren't sure what book he was talking about.

"I was intrigued," said Ivan, defiant without being disrespectful.

"Indeed." Mikalus swept across the room, and by that I mean I wasn't really sure if he walked or floated. Definitely some vampire action going on there.

I kept silent as he came, studying him, filing it all away to add to my meager knowledge of these strange, secretive creatures. Ivan was the only vamp I knew, the only one I'd ever known to speak more than a few words to, and I hadn't seen Mikalus since I'd inadvertently helped resurrect the most powerful ex-human on the planet. Which is an accomplishment of sorts, I guess.

He was still slender, but no longer skinny, just slim and healthy looking in a vampiric, otherworldly way. Meaning, he was pale—no sun for this guy, that hadn't ended well last time—making his eyes seem sunken, his fingers were bony, the nails that little bit too long and pointy to be normal as he was old skool and they all did that back in the day, and his straight black hair hung low and lustrous. All in all he looked exactly how you'd expect the leader of the vampires to look. He also had seriously cool taste in clothes.

Meaning, he wore sagging, washed-out jeans with a frayed leather belt, a black vest showing off his strong muscles, and was barefoot. My kind of guy as he looked like I would if I was an immortal vampire and had access to nice hair products. Plus a razor.

"Nice to see you again, Arthur." Mikalus stopped a few feet away and smiled at me and Ivan. I tried not to think about how he'd got in; the door certainly hadn't opened, I'd have seen it if it did.

"You too. Been keeping busy?"

"Oh, you know, this and that." Mikalus waved it all away with a languid swish of the hand.

"Feeling, er, all right after your rebirth?" Look, it was difficult to think what to say, okay?

"Actually, I feel fabulous. Better than I ever did. This new world, it's so different to the old ways. So much to learn, so much to see and do. And the people, they are more open than back in my time. It's nice to not have to be so circumspect. Did you know, in my time I was seen as somewhat of a problem? A pariah. Our kind had to hide or risk terrible punishment. Now there are those willing to... Ah, but I digress. Yes, I am well. And you?"

"Good, all good. Although, this book you wanted has caused me a lot of trouble. You know who it really belongs to, right?"

Mikalus nodded and took a step closer. He smelled funny. Sweet, almost cloying, but earthy too, although I didn't for one minute believe he rested in a dirt-lined coffin during the day. Although, he was from a different time after all. He was intoxicating, his essence made me feel funny inside and his power was almost overwhelming. That would be the immortal blood coursing through his veins. Assuming it did course, I guess, but it would have to, wouldn't it? Otherwise, he'd have feet full of blood, same as all the other vamps. I decided there and then I'd make it my goal to learn all I could about vampires.

They were, whether I liked it or not, going to play a large part in my future. I knew that, so I had to understand them.

"I know. That's why I had Ivan employ the very best. You."

"I'm flattered. But also a little pissed."

"Arthur, show some respect!" hissed Ivan.

I scowled at him then turned back to Mikalus and said, "With all due respect, I'm a little pissed. This angel nearly killed me, several times, and he's ruined my evening. And my car. A heads-up would have been nice."

"I apologize. Aurelius can be quite a handful. Mostly harmless though, as long as you keep your cool. That's what they say isn't it? Keep your cool?"

"Yeah, it is. And I did, mostly. But like I said, I could have been warned about what I'd be up against."

"Ah, so you wanted every piece of information I had on the book? To know exactly what would happen and how dangerous it might be?" Mikalus stared deep into my eyes, and I felt a little funny, lightheaded and off-guard. Was he trying to glamor me? Motherfucker! I fortified my mind with magic that slammed down like a solid barrier, and eyeballed him right back. Take that, old man.

"Yeah, something like that," I mumbled.

"And is that how it usually works? Or do you get given a job and go do it regardless of the risk?"

"Depends," I muttered. This was getting me nowhere. "Look, all I'm saying is that I should have been told this angel, Aurelius, wanted the book. He manifest and almost killed me."

"And then you understood he fed on your fear, your energy, your willingness, your desire to do him harm, and he was gone, yes?"

"Right," I nodded.

"Then all is well. Thank you for the book. I assume you have been paid?"

"I havc."

"Good. Then that is all."

I knew when I was being dismissed, so, rather than do anything I'd regret, I nodded, glanced at the book, then made to leave.

Mikalus picked up the book and held it gently in his hands. "Arthur, don't you want to know what this is?" he asked, waving it at me.

"Nope. You paid, I delivered, our business is done. For good."

"As you wish. Farewell."

"See you."

My body screaming at me to run the hell away, I stayed calm, moved like I was Mr. Chilled, even did the gangster shoulder roll. Just a few more minutes and I was out of here. Door open, I glanced up.

"Oh, seriously? Now? C'mon!"

"Hello, Arthur," said Carmichael.

Introductions

"And you are?" asked Ivan, his breath warm on my neck he was so close.

Mikalus was the other side of me, so we blocked the doorway. Damn, they were fast.

"Allow me to introduce myself. I'm Carmichael." The new head of Cerberus, or the face of Cerberus anyway, smiled pleasantly and offered his hand. Surprisingly, Mikalus took it, and Ivan moved closer as if to protect him. Carmichael seemed to know who was in charge, and there was something else, a vibe, like this was somehow pretense.

Carmichael frowned down at his left hand, where he held a slender case. It was cracked, the wood broken, runes covering it damaged. He pocketed it.

Carmichael angled his head so he could peek into the apartment; his eyes widened when he saw the book on the counter. "Ah, I see Arthur here came through on his promise."

"He's a very adept young man." I liked that, it wasn't often, make that ever, that I got called young.

"He is, shall we say, very enterprising. Caused a little trouble lately, haven't you, Arthur? He killed my predecessor, blew up a helicopter, saw things he ought not to see."

"My, my, you have been busy," said Mikalus, smiling at me. Neither he nor Ivan moved from the doorway.

I figured it best not to mention the dead goons in the hall, everyone could see them as well as I could. "Um, well, I'll leave you to it then," I said, deciding I definitely needed a holiday.

"Stay awhile," said Mikalus, putting a hand to my shoulder. He didn't squeeze hard, but there was plenty implied by the way he placed his hand. I felt the strength he had, that he could crush my shoulder into dust.

"Sure, sounds nice. Can't think of a better way to spend the evening." I backed up, then decided that if this was how these fuckers wanted to play it, their stupid games of one-upmanship, then so be it. Me, I was going to stay as far out of it as I could. Which wasn't far enough at all, but we don't always get what we want. In fact I hardly ever do.

I wandered over to the posh sofa and slumped down onto the steel and leather contraption. It was about as comfortable as straddling a saddle made of nails. Naked. Nevertheless, I reclined, draped an arm over the back, and watched the show.

"Please, come in," said Mikalus, nodding to Ivan. They stepped away, and Mikalus swept a hand inward for Carmichael to enter. I had to hand it to him, he remained cool, calm, and collected as he shook hands again with the First, and then with the most dangerous gangster in the country.

He made a beeline straight for the book but Mikalus was there well before him, that freaky floating, walking thing again. "Come now, you are my guest. It would be a shame for you to overstep the bounds of my hospitality." No mention was made of what Carmichael and Cerberus must have gone through to get inside, although the lack of heavy gunfire or magic in the air made me question if this was a raid or he'd got in by more nefarious means, only using violence outside the door. These damn guys, so bloody sneaky.

"I apologize, old habits and all that." Carmichael stepped away from the counter and stood at ease, eyes dancing, smiling like he knew something we all didn't. "I must say, you're a hard man to meet. Did you get our messages?"

"Do you mean the corpses, or the Hounds you sent to inquire as to a meeting?"

"Ah, yes, well, the more violent approach was preferred by my predecessor, but I run things for the time being. Let's start again, shall we? Wipe the past out and begin on a more pleasant footing? A clean slate."

"That sounds preferable," said Mikalus. "So, young Arthur has been causing you some trouble has he?"

"More than a little. But he'll come around."

"I bloody won't."

"Has he seen the warehouse?" asked Mikalus.

Carmichael's eyes darkened, then he laughed. "He has. You are well-informed, it seems. Nobody knows about the warehouse."

"I do." Mikalus pointed to the sofas, and Carmichael nodded. Then they were all sitting, me next to Carmichael, the vampires opposite.

This was getting too weird. What was going on here? They acted like they were old friends. Playing games as though they knew each other and were pretending they didn't.

I studied each man as the silence extended. They were relaxed, not acting, but calm, and the way they looked at each other made it seem like they'd met many times before.

"Who are you?" I asked Carmichael. "And enough with the bullshit. What's this all about?"

"I'm the new acting head of Cerberus. I told you. And this is about you, and Mikalus, interfering in our business." Carmichael turned away from me and faced Mikalus. "It's been quiet with you gone, and our work has mostly been a success, but your return has ruffled a few feathers, has people concerned. Even him. He is not amused by your escalation of activity, and your obsession with so many artifacts. It has to stop, old friend. You cannot have this book. You cannot let it happen again."

Aha, there it was. Old friend. What was the deal here? Ivan and I exchanged a glance. He was as much in the dark as I was. Let what happen again? Just what the hell was this book?

"It must be done. Surely you understand?" said Mikalus, sympathy for Carmichael tinging his words, as if he understood the importance of this.

"We do not. He does not. I sympathize, but when you were gone our work proceeded apace. Those tasked with running Cerberus mostly did a good job, although we have had more casualties lately than in many years." Carmichael glanced at me, then back to Mikalus. "You are a disruption, and we cannot, will not, let this happen. For old time's sake, hand over the book."

"No, I cannot. You understand its importance, know what it means, so don't ask again."

"You know he won't stand for this," said Carmichael.

"He? Who's he?" I asked.

"The head of Cerberus," said Carmichael, as if talking to a child. "He, our boss I suppose you would call him, has made it his life's work to stop magic ruining this world, and any other, and that means keeping the Nolands separate from earth. Magic doesn't belong here, it belongs there. It is our duty to stop this world breaking down. Mikalus wishes to ruin it all. I cannot allow it. He will not allow it."

"Oh, right, well, that's that all cleared up." I sank back into the sofa, everything more confusing than ever. I hated all this stuff, these games with words, these power plays and subtle gestures and actions that the top guys thrived on. It was all bullshit, but they loved this crap.

Mikalus leaned forward, angry. "Tell him I'll do as I please. I answer to no one. I will have this, I will do it, and there is nothing you can do to stop me."

Carmichael rose. "So be it. This was a friendly visit, a reminder if you like, but it will not be repeated. Good to see you. Again. You look different. Better in this age. This century suits you."

"As it does you," said Mikalus, rising too.

Carmichael nodded, glanced at Ivan and me, then left.

"Well, guess I'll be off too. Nice meeting you again. Thanks for the job, next time offer it to someone else."

"As you wish. And Arthur?"

"Yeah?"

"Don't go searching for answers. It won't lead anywhere you want it to. Forget what you heard in this room. It's for your own good."

"Wouldn't dream of it. Mum's the word. Can't remember a thing." I nodded at both men, then I left too.

The corridor was empty, Carmichael was gone. What the fuck was that all about?

Walking the Streets

I took a nice circuitous route back to my semi, parked a few streets away, then went for a wander. I had a lot to think about, and I honestly didn't know where to start. At least the book was gone; that was something.

What was all that crap with Carmichael and Mikalus? They knew each other? From the past? But Mikalus had been missing in action for several hundred years, and when alive had been living off in some remote European country. Probably in a crumbling castle in the middle of nowhere where he got a local virgin delivered by the townsfolk once a month so he didn't go nuts and devour them all. He was ancient, from a different time and world, so how did Carmichael know him?

When you're faced with questions that only have one logical answer then it's usually right. Meaning, Carmichael, the new, posh, identikit face of Cerberus, and it really made me wonder who the actual boss was, this "He" they both talked about, was at least several centuries old. He was either a vampire himself, but I didn't get that vibe from him, plus he didn't fade from memory like most vamps did, or a very powerful magic user in his own right. Much more powerful then I'd believed. Yeah, it was staring right at me.

Carmichael, the man in charge of ensuring magic users didn't get their hands on magical items, was a fucking ancient wizard. How about that for irony?

The two men clearly had a history. They'd dealt with each other. Probably because of Mikalus' penchant for forbidden books. Aha, something clicked. I bet when Mikalus got the old death by sun, Cerberus were there pretty damn quick to swipe his library. No wonder he was pissing them off so much going after all these books. Maybe some had somehow been sold on, you get dodgy types in every organization and I bet over a few hundred years a few Hounds had taken books and sold them on for a nice sum, or maybe Mikalus' library had been looted before Cerberus got there and most of it was still in circulation.

Yes, I was getting somewhere. Mikalus was reclaiming his lost library, Cerberus had some of his books, and both parties were annoyed at the other for what each saw as taking a right liberty. And, they both seemed to know quite a lot about Aurelius, and what the book contained. What was it? I racked my brains as I walked past silent houses, down alleys where cats and rats ran from my presence, oblivious to most of it as I was lost deep in thought. What was the game here? What were they up to?

I found myself on a nice wide street, almost an avenue, one where detached houses had large landscaped gardens and the road was split in two by a central grassy divide with willows and beech trees sucking up the fumes of the city to keep the residents healthy.

My phone vibrated in my pocket and I fished it out. I had a serious number of missed calls, like an epic number. Instantly, my heart leaped into my mouth. Was there something wrong at home? Had Vicky done something stupid? No, it was Ivan. What the hell did he want? I wasn't going to work for them any more.

"Yeah?"

"Do you have it? I'm assuming it wasn't you?" He sounded stressed. Very, very stressed.

"What are you talking about?"

"The book!" he shouted. "It got switched. Did he slip it to you?"

"Who? What's going on?"

Ivan took a deep breath then said, "Carmichael switched the book. We just looked at it, it's blank. Empty. It's fake. Carmichael must have switched it. Did he slip it to you? Check your pockets?"

"If he switched it why would he give it to me? He'd just take it."

"No, he wouldn't. Because he didn't have anything to contain it in. He and the book, or the angel, go way back apparently. Mikalus said the angel would be on him in an instant if he had it, so chances are he hid it on you so he could come collect when he had a secure box to put it in, stop it from being located. Check your pockets!" Ivan was practically screaming at me, and he was always cool.

"Fine. But you're barking up the wrong tree here. Hang on." I fumbled with my phone, patted my jeans, knowing I'd have felt it, then my jacket pockets, of which there were several. One of the side ones, almost invisible with the way the material was designed, as a wizard can never have too many pockets and sometimes I even lost things in my clothes, felt hard, like there was a book inside.

Frowning, I checked, and sure enough I pulled out the book. "Motherfucker."

"You have it?"

"Yeah, that bastard slipped it in."

"Don't move, we'll be there in a few minutes."

"Wait, how do you know where I am?" Ivan hung up. I knew how he'd know. The bloody technological age. It was why I kept my sim and phone separate if I remembered, but I kept forgetting. You could track anything, and phones were easy, especially if you had enough cash to buy all the gear necessary to trace them. Vicky had explained it all, and thank God she had, otherwise I'd have been about as easy to find as a giraffe in the city center. Maybe I should go back to carrying coins and using phone booths? But then I worried I'd miss a call if George was in trouble, so instead just made a mental note to be extra careful about when I used it.

Still frowning at the book, and with my phone in the other hand, I almost dropped them both as a black sedan screeched around the corner and sped toward me.

The car skidded to a halt and I shouted, "That was quick," right before someone started shooting at me.

Just When You Think You're Out

"These bastards always suck me back in," I muttered as I ducked behind a tree. Pulpy flesh exploded where my head was a moment ago, and I shuffled sideways and sucked in my belly, apologizing to the tree that was fast becoming toothpicks. Keeping behind the trunk, I pocketed the phone, begrudgingly put the book away somewhere safe, and pulled out my wand.

Sigils flared, almost as angry as I was, and magic crackled, sending a familiar vibration running up my arm. Ah, so sweet, this magic I'd fought so hard to call my own. Well, they picked the wrong day, and the wrong pissed off wizard, to pull this crap on. I just wanted some peace, I wanted some cake. I wanted some love.

With naughty images of a naked Candy and plenty of chocolate cake distracting me, I smiled, then felt nervous, not about the guys with guns, but about asking Candy if she'd like me to lick cake off her... Ugh, what was wrong with me? Terrified of asking for a date, just annoyed about dudes shooting at me. Something definitely skewy there. Still, the image lingered, and it gave me hope.

"Sorry about that, Arthur, my men got a little carried away." It was Carmichael, the snake.

"Yeah, well, don't let it happen again. You tricked me, that's not nice." I risked a glance into the street and saw Carmichael standing beside the car, two goons with guns aimed at me. What was with them? This was a residential street, Cerberus didn't usually act like this. Carmichael really wanted this fucking book.

"Hand it over, then we'll go. You've got about a minute before Aurelius arrives, so now would be a good time."

"Fuck you, and fuck your Hounds. What, you okay with bullets flying while citizens are sleeping? You woke them up, you fucktards. Gonna carry on shooting?" Haha, I had them right where I wanted them now.

In answer, a single shot was fired. Then another, then another. All the street lights were out. But already light was spilling out onto the large front lawns as people woke up and pulled back the curtains.

"I want it. You don't understand."

"Tough. It's Mikalus' now, take it up with him."

"I warned you."

Guns blazed in suburbia. I sucked my belly in further and decided there was only one thing for it. I let rip, fired a Hat special at the dark shadows of the Hounds and Carmichael. Which is all well and good when you can aim properly, but I kind of fired off the wand by reaching out my hand and hoping it was pointing in the right direction. Magic flared, blinding light lit up the street, and then an almighty explosion set off car alarms and smashed windows.

I peeked and said, "Oops," as I got a face full of heat. I'd only gone and blown up the car. Something moved, and I watched Carmichael get to his feet and brush himself down. The two Hounds were either dead or unconscious.

"That was rather extreme," noted Carmichael, as he advanced, tweed suit singed and smoking, but acting like he didn't have a care in the world. The air shimmered around him as though he were protected with a magical forcefield, silver sparks darting off.

"I'm stressed," I said. For some reason, I didn't try to blast him to bits, just watched as he walked toward me as the car burned, more curtains were opened, and the sound of sirens grew closer.

Carmichael stopped several feet away and held out his hand. "Give it to me. Last warning."

I smiled, heard the noise behind as the car came to a halt, and said, "Not this time."

Another screech of tires, another series of doors opening. More footsteps, and more unwanted company. Although, maybe this would finally be over.

"Ivan sent us," said one of two very large goons that took a place either side of me.

"Good. He didn't come himself?"

"He's the boss," said the other.

"Course he is. Wouldn't want to ruin his suit."

Carmichael stared from me to the goons and back again. He raised a perfect eyebrow and said, "Let's not make this difficult. Please, hand it over."

"Fuck you."

"What was that? What's happening," screamed a goon as blackness descended and feathers floated wildly on the drafts caused by the fire.

"Chill out. Don't get freaked." I warned. But it was too late. The goons, not ones accustomed to much of the supernatural, glanced around nervously and waved very large guns this way and that. I knew it wouldn't do any good, but there was no stopping them.

They fired off into the shadowy shape that eddied around us, too fast for the eye to follow. I noted with interest that Carmichael was already retreating down the road.

"Oh no you don't," I shouted, and I ran after him as the goons began to scream.

I turned in time to witness Aurelius manifest with all the drama he had last time, great raven wings spreading wide as his naked perfection confused and scared the goons. The worse they got, the more solid he became, and then they screamed in earnest as the life seemcd to drain out of them. Aurelius advanced, he spread his wings wider, then engulfed them in an instant. Then he was up and away, soaring above them as his body became ephemeral. They dropped down, terrified looks frozen on their faces, and very, very dead.

Note to self. Don't freak out in front of angels, they'll suck you dry.

Carmichael was still hightailing it so I chased after him, following the sound of his hand-crafted leather shoes tapping against asphalt that had been free of damage until we showed up.

Then he did something pretty fucking cool. He pulled a round object the size of a lacrosse ball from his pocket, except it was way too shiny for that sport or any other, and then a starless rectangle opened up in front of him. He ran headlong at it and disappeared.

As the oblong shrank, I launched, sailed through the air, and dove right through into the emptiness just as it closed behind me.

Strange

Pain, a very familiar pain, detonated as I felt my existence torn away then reassembled piece by piece. Ah, the joys of going through portals. I was used to it, but when you aren't geared up for such a trip it still comes as one hell of a shock. At least it was quick, although a fraction of a second of excruciating agony as you are disassembled then rebuilt atom by atom in a timeless nothingness can feel like a lifetime, trust me on that.

I was still diving when I emerged on the other side, so I tucked my head in, rolled forward, and took a glancing blow off something solid. Momentum carried me forward and I only stopped when I smashed into a wall of books. I pushed back, ready to do something nasty, but stopped as something caught my eye. Fascinated, surprised, and excited simultaneously, I turned my head sideways to better read the spine. Impressed, I glanced in every direction, taking it all in. Many books had no titles, most didn't in fact, and I had wits enough to ensure I kept my hands well away from them as the magical emanations tried to suck me forward.

Even forcibly trying to control them, my hands moved of their own accord and I reached out, only just taking a step back in time before I was pulling rare magical books from the shelves as their incessant whispers clawed at my mind and acted like a drug.

"Hands off if you don't mind."

Back to reality, I spun and found Carmichael replacing a lamp I must have knocked off an antique side table.

"Huh?" was all I managed, my mind not quite caught up with what was happening.

"Don't touch. Lots of nasty things in there. You get used to it, and they calm down once they know you aren't going to just open them without putting up protection. Now, would you mind leaving? Oh, and the book please? Now isn't the time, or the place, to play around, Arthur."

Carmichael turned serious, almost angry, and he held out his hand.

"No chance."

"Do you knew where you are? Who you are dealing with?"

"No, and no. And I don't care. You used me, then your guys shot at me. You risked citizens."

"A mistake, one for which the men have already paid, thanks to you. I was in a hurry, and they were the only Hounds close by."

"Excuses, excuses. And what the fuck was that? You opened a portal. How?"

"Obvious. I summoned it. Used something only a few of us can use." Carmichael fidgeted in his pocket with his other hand. The artifact he'd used.

"Wouldn't mind one of those myself."

"Shame you don't have one then." Carmichael thrust his free hand further forward, and I almost wavered, almost gave it to him just to be done with the whole thing. This damn book was like a loyal puppy, following me everywhere I went. But I wouldn't be done with this mess, even if I gave the book to Carmichael, would I? Mikalus had paid, it was his. But I have to say I was tempted.

"You're such a hypocrite, same as all the others before you. You don't want anyone else to have any artifacts, want to control magic, but you are happy using them yourself, playing with toys if you want to. So full of shit."

"There's a monumental difference between using something powerful with proper respect, and owning something you shouldn't own and risking untold damage. You know that."

"Spare me. We've had this conversation before and I still think you're all a bunch of control freaks. You want to own us, you want to control everything. You don't get to decide who's worthy. You sure as shit aren't."

I studied the room best I could whilst still keeping an eye on Carmichael. His office, I assumed. There was a desk, oak with green leather insert, walls and walls of priceless books, a number of interesting bits and pieces, some of which were artifacts, others merely rare objects, all to do with magic, and filing cabinets, paintings, antiques, all the trappings of a rich man working for a powerful, super-secret organization. It made me want to throw up. It was all very plush, very nice, very exactly where you'd expect a posh secret agent to while away the hours between hobnobbing with politicians and planning how to rule the world because he felt he had the right.

"We at Cerberus HQ again?"

"How did you guess? Such powers of observation you have."

"Haha, very funny. Now, if you're finished blathering, I'll be leaving."

"You, my troublesome friend, are going nowhere."

"Wanna bet?"

And with that, I blasted the shit out of his wall of priceless books. Okay, I was selective, and okay, it was an illusion, no harm done, but he didn't know that. As a wall of fire erupted, although there was no heat, Carmichael panicked, just for a few seconds, and as he recoiled in horror, what little color there was draining from his face, which made me incredibly happy, I changed up the magic. This time it was real, and deadly.

I blasted him hard. He was fast, and had protection, but it still sent him flailing. The small object he had in his hand went rolling across the oak floor and stopped as it hit a thick rug. I lunged for it.

Carmichael was fast though, and he landed on my back, taking the wind out of me. I jabbed out with an elbow, felt ribs, and did it again, harder. Then I rolled sideways, slammed down into his stomach, and as he gasped for air and his face turned puce I scrambled for this precious artifact he was so keen to hold on to and grabbed it tight. It was cool, but obviously incredibly powerful, something dangerous yet rare and pure at the same time.

Carmichael grabbed me by the ankle as I moved to stand, and I slammed down onto his expensive rug. I kicked out, managed to boot him in the face, and smiled as I heard cartilage crunch. Then, without looking back at him, I jumped up, opened the door, and ran away.

That'd teach him. It was just a shame I was running away in Cerberus HQ, which was becoming a nasty habit and one I definitely had to break.

Yes!

I sprinted down a flag-stoned corridor, with cut stone walls, a red carpet runner softening my footsteps. I was definitely in Cerberus HQ, I recognized the style of build and the plush, understated decor. There was a timelessness to this place, like it had been a seat of power for centuries. Inherited wealth and civic duty, political machinations, and a sense of righteousness practically oozed from the very fabric of the building. I hated it.

Ignoring the funny looks, knowing it was only a short matter of time before I got gooned again, I checked out what I was holding.

"No fucking way."

It was a Teleron, fabled ultra-artifact. I hadn't believed they existed, had heard of them the same as all wizards, but never seen one. This was, like, utterly awesome. I thought about all the stories I'd heard, about how this was basically a shortcut through the Nolands, using the forces contained within that dimension to draw magic and take you instantly from one place to the next. You just had to focus, and focus clearly, and there you were, like stepping through the Nolands without actually going through it. If that makes sense?

What we had here was an incredibly powerful, finely crafted, upmarket, definitely more compact version of my gates. You weren't restricted to one entry and exit point, you could use it anywhere, go anywhere you knew intimately. The way I'd heard it worked was that you had to have a very clear image in your mind of where you wanted to go, somewhere familiar. Otherwise, and here was the catch, you'd kind of end up as mush. It might not give you the freedom to appear anywhere in the world, but it sure beat getting a taxi.

So, without further ado, I twisted the brass ring around the center of the small steel ball, closed my eyes, thought real hard, then opened them. An infinitely deep, colorless rectangle appeared several paces ahead, so, still running, and without pausing to worry about this going wrong, as if it did I would be chatting with Death in the next second, I dove right through.

Are You Kidding?

I rolled, came to a halt on my feet, and brushed myself down. I turned, only to find myself staring down the barrel of a gun. Excited and hyped, I grinned.

"Arthur!"

"Thought I'd find you here," I said, relieved when Ivan lowered the gun.

"How did you do that?" he asked, wide-eyed but relaxing when he realized I was alone.

"Aha, wizardly secrets." I pocketed the Teleron, definitely not something to advertise. I could just imagine the look on Carmichael's face, and unless he happened to have another one stashed away he was gonna have to come visit me the long way round. That would take hours. No wonder these guys managed to arrive so quickly, right when you didn't want them to.

"How did you know I was here?" he asked, slumping into his chair.

"I knew you'd want something familiar, something real. Something more seedy. We're from this world, not that one," I said, looking around his spartan office, a room I'd been in on many occasions, stared at enough times, for it to be familiar.

"It does feel more natural. I'll have to move away from the apartment. I feel like an impostor there. Mikalus won't like it, but he'll understand."

"Well, good for you. Look, that's all great and all, but can we please, pretty please, with sugar on top, finish this bloody deal?"

"Absolutely. Mikalus was furious when we noticed the switch. He said you'd have the book, that Carmichael, that snake, wouldn't want it until he was ready."

"Because that box he had with him was broken? It was to mask the book, wasn't it?"

"Yes."

"Right, to business. And this time, nothing better go wrong." I dropped the book on the table, and then, saying nothing, not caring if Ivan had a way to get it to Mikalus or not, I turned and I bloody well left him to it.

Without incident, I walked away, and kept on walking, until I finally felt free of the whole sordid business. But something kept nagging at me, as though there was unfinished business, and try as I might, I couldn't shake the feeling that this was far from over. It was a familiar feeling, as these things seldom had a satisfactory conclusion. There were always more loose ends and nothing was ever done and dusted. Still, I lived in hope.

I must have walked for ten minutes before I heard the boom. I glanced back, only to see a huge fire raging in the distance. No prizes for guessing where it was coming from. I turned my back on it, and I kept on walking.

This wasn't my problem, it was Ivan's. If Aurelius was there, which he obviously was, then this was down to Ivan and his guys, not me. I'd played my part, done more than I had to. Had delivered the book several times now, so it wasn't my fault if they couldn't keep hold of the damn thing.

Time for The Hat to go home and toss and turn in his bed, another job done, if not exactly well. They were all grown men, they could sort it out amongst themselves.

I stopped, turned back to face the fire, and swore. "I better get a fucking bonus." Then I ran back toward what I was certain would be more of the same old bullshit.

No Respite

It was, to say the least, carnage.

The factory was ablaze, an inferno that raged and had already caught the smaller buildings, the piles of crap everywhere, the old conveyor belts and anything else even slightly flammable.

The night was fierce with heat and fire, but I saw nobody.

Not a good sign.

It was kind of sad to think Ivan was gone. He had his faults, and there were plenty of them, but he was better than any other boss before him, better than what would come next, I was sure. Plus, I almost liked him, and he was Vicky's family. Hell, he didn't even know what had happened, did he? What Vicky had done? Guess he never would now.

I squinted at the flames, at the collapsed building as the fire began to burn itself out. Already there was little flammable remaining, just steel and brick.

I watched, half surprised, half not, as a black silhouette strode out from the flames.

Ivan was scorched black, his hair gone along with his clothes, but as he marched forward, leaving the conflagration behind, and as ash fell and fire crackled, his skin healed, his hair grew back, just stubble, and by the time he reached me he was whole for the most part. His skin shone strangely, too pink and raw, and he looked funny without the nice hair, but he was okay.

"Damn, perks of being a vampire."

"Maybe, but it really hurts." Ivan screamed, his face locked in a spasm of pain, and he toppled forward, the shock of it all too much for his mind to take even if his body had handled it.

He still held the book.

"This bloody book," I moaned, and, call it intuition, call it just what I didn't want to happen, or my wizardly luck kicking in, I dropped down flat next to Ivan's steaming body as an angel of immortal persistence swept over us.

Miffed that Ivan had been so badly damaged, and cursing the book, the angel, and everything else in my life, I whipped out old faithful and let the magic surge. Forked death spasmed from the wand and flared bright as it arced and crackled into the fiery night. But even when it hit the angry cloud of the semi-formed angel all it did was splat it into smaller wispy clouds that coalesced angrily, slamming tight into each other as if for strength.

I tried something different, sending a volley of small balls of darkest intent at Aurelius, not so much blasts as packets of absence of anything, magic that few could use, and even fewer successfully. As pockets of emptiness littered the air like miniature black holes, I thought maybe I'd found a way to defeat this immortal being. Small sections of the spreading cloud spun wildly, spiraling around and into the emptiness I created, but then the ripples reversed and spat out what had been consumed. Then, suddenly, my magic was gone, sucked away by something beyond such parlor tricks.

Even though I knew it was futile, I had to try, and I had to stay calm. I let a stillness wash over me as I stood amid the heat and flame and an angel whizzed angrily about my head. The calmer I grew, the more spread out the cloud of Aurelius became, dispersing like mist evaporating on a summer's day. I wondered if maybe he'd soon dissipate entirely, or at least be utterly ineffective. But then he drew power from somewhere, maybe from Ivan who was groaning on the ground, back from the dead.

Then he was solid, and he was there above me in all his celestial glory. Wings spread wide, arms outstretched, legs tight together, like the perfect Vitruvian man, just with feathers and nicer hair. He descended without a single strand of that lovely hair blowing out of place or a feather being ruffled, like the real world didn't count for him.

He alighted right onto Ivan's back. Bone crunched, Ivan gasped, his eyes went wide, and he screamed.

Aurelius grinned at me with perfect teeth like whitewashed tombstones, then lifted his head to stare at the stars. He raised his arms higher as if calling down heavenly forces, and damn if the bloody world didn't implode. Everything was white. White blinding my eyes, white noise making my ears ring, everything all soft and like cotton wool had been stuffed inside me.

Then I was back to my senses, feeling alien and out of my body, as though I'd been touched by something truly timeless and godlike. I shook my head to get the thoughts moving and then I lost the use of my legs. I ended up prone before Aurelius, kneeling on the ashes of the destruction he'd caused, helpless to resist. I fell forward, even though I swear I didn't want to. His power was at its peak, the chaos and violence of the chase for the book having reached a crescendo.

Aurelius looked down on me and I looked up at him, knowing this was over.

Ivan was out cold, unaware of what was happening. Aurelius ground a foot into his back; he could crush him like a bug if he wanted to, kill him for good.

With no other choice, I grabbed the undamaged book from Ivan's hand, and scrabbled to my feet.

"Okay, fine, you win," I shouted. "Have the bloody thing." I waved the book in the air and waited.

Aurelius shot up like a celestial rocket then swept down from the sky, silhouetted by flame, and landed delicately beside Ivan. His wings folded and he held out his hand. I reached forward with the book, and as he took hold our fingers touched.

With my other hand in my pocket, I turned the dial, focused real hard, trying to get as clear an image as possible, then leapt forward as the portal opened silently behind this most insistent nemesis, pushing Aurelius and myself through.

I landed on top of him, but jumped to my feet before he had chance to understand what had happened. I turned to Carmichael, sitting behind his desk, talking on the phone, a bandage over his nose, and said, "Don't say I never give you anything." Moments later, well before anyone had time to do much of anything apart from gawp, I was outta there, leaving the angel behind.

Let 'em work it out between them. They obviously had a history, whatever that was, and I felt sure that at least they'd both be out of my hair for a while. It was all over in a second, and then I was twiddling again and back at the factory, bending over Ivan to check he would make it.

Feeling strangely apprehensive, I rolled him over. He was fine. From a height higher than strictly necessary, I dropped the book onto his belly, nodded at the goons converging on him, and told them, "Tell Mikalus The Hat always delivers."

Then I walked away, again, and this time I didn't turn around, just kept walking all the way back to my semi, removing my sim as I walked. I went in, stepped through the portal, drove home, and it was only as I pulled up at the farmhouse that I remembered I could have used the Teleron.

But I was a creature of habit, and I liked my gates. Plus, to be honest, the Teleron freaked me out too much. It wasn't like I knew how my gates worked, but they were big, and solid, and we had history. The

Teleron just felt a little too much like taking chances, and you know me, I don't like taking risks.

Boots off, wards checked, I wandered wearily into the kitchen.

George was up, coffee was brewing.

"You look awful. And is that smoke I smell?" she asked.

"Yeah, but it's not mine. Same as last time."

"Busy night?"

"Usual. Pour us a coffee, there's a love."

George poured me a coffee and brought it over to the table. I sipped, letting the bitterness scald my throat. "Aah, that's so good."

"Better drink up, it's going to be a loud morning."

"Huh?"

"Our guests," she said.

And with that, I heard Vicky shouting at the girls, the girls running around, having obviously taken to wearing traditional wooden Dutch clogs, and then they stomped down the stairs like two baby elephants.

Hell came to my kitchen in the form of a stressed, haggard looking mother, and two children who wanted cereal, and toast, and sticky things on said toast. Now, right now.

Purgatory truly is having untidy house guests. It's the worst.

Here Goes

I pushed open the door, feeling sick to my stomach. My guts churned, threatening to erupt in the nastiest of ways. Sharp pains stabbed at my stomach as though an evil wizard was prodding me right through with a fizzing wand.

The little bell above the door jangled and with it my nerves. I jumped, glanced up, and muttered something foul under my breath. As the door closed behind me, I removed my hat and wiped at my sweating brow. Bloody hell, I hadn't felt so scared since that time I found myself staked out in a forest in deepest Sumatra while a local witch doctor danced around me in his birthday suit and giant red ants direct from the Nolands clicked their mandibles and headed for my private parts that were, against all protestations, coated with honey.

In fact, this was worse. I felt my testicles shrink up so small and tight I wondered if they'd ever drop down again, and as I put my hat back on I noticed my hands were shaking. I glanced around the small coffee shop, and waved awkwardly at Candy who looked up, nodded at me, then returned to whatever she was doing behind the counter.

"Arthur, hey, over here, mate." Steve nodded at me from a table jammed against the wall by the front window, all smiles and casual good looks.

I wandered over, every step feeling like I was sinking into quicksand. "Hey, Steve, how's it going?" I asked.

"Fine, mate. You all right? Looking a bit green there. Been a busy night?"

"Um, no, not really. Not busy I mean. I'm feeling just dandy." Dandy? Who the hell says dandy? Not wizards in their forties, that's for sure. "Um, look, sorry to hear about you not keeping the job with the vampires. Ivan said he just wanted to cut out the middleman."

"Yeah, gotta say, I was pissed when he told me. But it's all good," he said brightly. "Got something better going on. This rich dude needed a bodyguard. Dabbles in a bit of the old magic, and some collecting, and he pays real good. I should hook you up some time, he's always on the lookout for anything interesting."

"Yeah, sounds good," I said, distracted by Candy stacking cups and saucers.

"You sure you're okay? You're really jumpy." Steve, badger shifter and probably the closest thing I had to a real guy friend, leaned forward, checking me out.

All I could think of was how handsome he was, how well groomed. With his hipster hairstyle and beard with more product than I felt was right, his casual manliness, the way his shirt hung and the way his jeans hugged muscular legs, it all made me realize how unkempt and scrawny I was.

I'd tried to spruce myself up, I really had. Showered, tamed the stubble, brushed my hair, even wore a nice brown shirt, and some jeans that cost way more than was right for simple denim sewn together, but the end result was the same. I was creased of clothes and face, looked like someone had stuck a nice hat and shirt on a scarecrow, and there was nothing I could do about it. This was me, and it wasn't a pretty sight. Sometimes I hated mirrors.

"Hello? Earth to Arthur." Steve waved a hand and I came back to myself.

"Sorry."

"Mate, you zoned out. You must be shattered. Not sleeping well?"

"Do I ever? Look, I need to have a word with Candy. But let's catch up soon, it's been too long. Weeks. Let's go grab a drink, or get something to eat? Sound good?"

"Yeah, sure thing, mate. I missed you actually. Haha." Steve pushed a hand through his hair; it glided with ease. If I tried that I'd spend the rest of the day trying to get my fingers back.

"Me too. I'll call." With a nod, I wandered off, wondering why it was so easy to make a date with a buddy but what I was about to do felt like the worst thing in the world.

The short walk, no more than a few steps from Steve to the counter, felt like a trek across a desert. My mouth went dry, my legs turned to jelly, and my guts really began to play up in earnest.

I struggled on, cursing and muttering to myself about how pathetic I was for stressing over such a simple thing. I was a man in my forties, I had a teenage daughter, I was a fucking wildcat wizard. A tough guy who beat down anyone who disrespected him. A man who had fought monsters without his heartbeat rising, who had killed more men and supernatural creatures than he could count, who had a bloody wand for crying out loud. Who owned not one, but two teleporters, who had more cash than he could spend, a very nice hat, and a lovely kitchen.

Get it together, Arthur, she'll just say no and you can laugh it off, say you understand as you're old and creased and she's young and gorgeous, and you can have a coffee and get over yourself.

At the counter, I stood there like a right lemon while Candy finished stacking crockery. I admired her bum in her tight black trousers, the way her hair fell on her shoulders, lost to dreams of what was beneath the white blouse, imagining touching her pale skin, and the delights of her warm body.

"You meeting someone? Ivan didn't say." Candy had finished and was staring at me funny. I must have zoned out again.

To say I got little sleep was an understatement, and it was only because Vicky and the girls were driving me so insane I wanted to scoop my brains out with a spoon that I'd even come at all.

"Me and Ivan are no longer business partners. Too full of surprises for my liking."

"Really? I thought you loved all that stuff." Candy's eyes sparkled, blue and clear, as inviting as a deep pool during a heatwave. Scary too. She was intense, confident, and a little intimidating. I loved it.

"Um, maybe." The silence extended, just a second or two but it felt like a lifetime.

"You okay? You look a funny color. Been on a job?"

"No, just slept badly. And Vicky and the girls aren't the quietest, or tidiest of house guests. I like my kitchen to sparkle, now it smells of sour milk and I keep finding weird things in odd places."

"Weird like what?"

"It said cheese on the packet, but it was shaped like a long spiral, and it was stuck under the table. I found the head of a doll, a very scary doll, in my dishwasher, and you should see my fridge. It's got strange stuff in it. Stuff in cartons and stuff with pictures of cartoon characters. Makes me feel old."

"Haha, that's kids for you. It's a good thing you did, Arthur, Vicky told me all about it. She's having a hard time, shame her husband went and got himself killed like that. You're a good friend."

Vicky had told Candy part of the story but obviously not all of it. She was still an utter mess after just a few days, but she was a survivor, her kids too.

"Maybe. But I'm running out of tea towels."

"A man after my own heart. I like things clean too."

"Yeah, I noticed. You wipe the counters more than I do."

Candy smiled at me, and I smiled back at her. It was now or never. I opened my mouth to blurt out something stupid and that I'd instantly regret but the door opened and a customer walked in.

I stepped aside while Candy served him. I honestly thought I was going to have a heart attack.

A Big Question

Candy wiped down the counter with a clean cloth after her customer had been served, then she leaned on her elbows and stared at me. The corners of her mouth were turned up in a bemused half-smile.

"Damn, you're scary."

"Gee, thanks."

"And gorgeous."

"I bet you say that to all the girls." She fluttered her eyelashes playfully, and I nearly lost what little control of my limbs I had left.

"I don't, I really don't. Look, um, I know I come across as a bit of a wise-ass. That I act like a bit of a... a..."

"A bit of an arrogant asshole?"

"Ugh, sorry. Do I really?"

"Sometimes. But mostly you're okay. You could do with toning down the intensity, but I guess that's just the way you are."

"Yeah, intense. Um, anyway, just wanted to say thanks for letting me use the place to deal with Ivan, I appreciate it."

"You're welcome. It's not like he didn't pay for the privilege." Candy took a half step back and put her hands on her wide, gorgeous hips. "Terrible at this, aren't you?" Smiling, she pushed her hair behind her ears and tugged her earlobe. I got palpitations.

"No, sorry. Um, I mean yes. Ugh, shall I start again?"

"If you like."

"And stop teasing me, I'm finding it hard to stay standing here."

"I didn't do a thing," she said, winking at me as she licked her lips. Goddamn!

I repeated a mantra silently as I studied her lovable face. Do not stare at her chest. Do not notice she has two buttons undone. Do not blow this. Candy just watched me, looking more amused by the second.

"Okay, look, here it is. I'm not a young dude, I'm kind of well worn, I'm trouble on legs. And I don't know the first thing about current music or movies or fashion or much that doesn't involve magic and gangsters."

"You sure know how to sell it."

"I know, right?" I said with a smile, "Who could resist?"

Candy frowned and I hurried on. "Sorry, there I go again. It's a defense mechanism when I'm nervous. I say stupid shit."

"I didn't think you got nervous. You, the heroic slayer of bad guys and all things supernatural." She looked genuinely surprised, but just goes to show.

"You'd be shocked at just how bad I'm feeling right now. I honestly thought about calling for an ambulance, my heart is going so crazy."

"Then spill it, mister. If you're going to ask what I think you're going to ask."

"That depends on whether you think I was going to ask you on a date, or, er, something else."

"Guess it does." Candy grinned; she really was making me squirm here.

"Candy, oh most beautiful woman I have ever met. Delight in a coffee shop. Would you do me the honor of accompanying me for a nice meal one evening so we can get to know each other better?"

"Why, when you flatter a girl like that, who could resist? I'd love to."

I let out a breath I think I'd been holding since I walked in the place, and said, "You would?"

"Sure, I like you. You're pretty hot, you know?"

"I am?"

"You are. All rugged and manly and like you know a thing or two." Candy's eyes sparkled. I don't think she was talking about knowing how to get a good table at a restaurant, although I knew how to do that too.

"Well, I have been around a while, learned a few tricks."

"Just one proviso."

"Okay," I said warily.

"Promise me you won't try to impress me. Just be yourself, no pretense."

"Honestly, I don't know any other way."

"Good, because neither do I. What you see is what you get."

I was about to say something stupid about liking what I saw and that I couldn't wait to get it, but figured that would be one of those things you say that gets you a slap and a canceled date, so instead I asked, "How about tonight?"

"That sounds fine. Seven. Meet me here?"

"You can count on it."

And with that, I smiled and walked out. I forgot to say goodbye to Steve, but I was sure he'd understand.

Outside the coffee shop, just around the corner and out of sight, I let the grin that had been forming loose, and smiled the first truly genuine smile I'd had in days.

People hurried past on their way to work, early shoppers squared their shoulders for some serious spending, and me, I ducked down into an alley, twisted the ring on the Teleron, and stepped out into my kitchen.

"That's it, you have to clean up, right now," I gasped as I took in the carnage.

Vicky turned and glared at me, then at the chaos, and then burst into tears.

George rushed in, babbling about Sasha having gone missing, my wards began to scream, some fault or other that happened now and then, the overloaded dishwasher smoked, rattled, then leaked soapy water all over the tiles, and a clearly insane woman prancing about in a leotard on Vicky's fitness workout show on the small TV shouted louder and louder for everyone to "Push it!"

Then the girls darted in, screaming about the bath overflowing, and as water dripped onto my hat through the ceiling, I just looked at my watch and counted down the hours until seven.

Just another day in the life of The Hat. But at least I had a date.

The End

Book 5, Honor Bound, coming soon.

Get author updates and new release notifications first via the Newsletter at www.alkline.co.uk.

Read the Dark Magic Enforcer series for more magical mayhem.

Printed in Great Britain
by Amazon

44650734R00177